PENGUIN BOOKS

TEXT FOR YOU

Sofie Cramer, born 1974 in Soltau, Germany, studied German and Political Science in Bonn and Hanover. At the beginning of her career she worked as an editor for radio. Today she lives near Hamburg and makes her living as an author, writing novels and developing stories for film and television. *Text for You* is her third novel, and the first that she wrote under a pseudonym—among other reasons because she chose to draw on her own personal experiences.

More on the author at www.sofie-cramer.de.

text for you

a novel

...

sofie cramer

penguin
books

PENGUIN BOOKS
An imprint of Penguin Random House LLC
penguinrandomhouse.com

First published in German as *SMS für dich* by Rowohlt
Taschenbuch Verlag, an imprint of Rowohlt
Verlag GmbH, Reinbek bei Hamburg.

LIBRARY OF CONGRESS CATALOGING-IN-PUBLICATION DATA
Names: Cramer, Sofie, 1974– author. | Yarbrough, Marshall, translator.
Title: Text for you : a novel / Sofie Cramer ;
[translated by Marshall Yarbrough].
Other titles: SMS für dich. English
Description: [New York] : Penguin Books, [2021] |
"First published in German as *SMS für dich* by Rowohlt Taschenbuch
Verlag, an imprint of Rowohlt Verlag GmbH, Reinbek bei Hamburg"
Identifiers: LCCN 2021038383 (print) | LCCN 2021038384 (ebook) |
ISBN 9780143136903 (paperback) | ISBN 9780525508380 (ebook)
Subjects: LCGFT: Romance fiction. | Novels.
Classification: LCC PT2707.O33 S6713 2021 (print) |
LCC PT2707.O33 (ebook) | DDC 833/.92—dc23
LC record available at https://lccn.loc.gov/2021038383
LC ebook record available at https://lccn.loc.gov/2021038384

Printed in the United States of America
1st Printing

Set in Wile Roman Pro
Designed by Alexis Farabaugh

For Björn

text
for
you

prologue

...

"Good morning, Lilime. Care for a croissant?"

Without opening her eyes, Clara breathes in the delightful aroma of fresh coffee. She stretches out on the soft bed and surrenders herself to the warm feeling that fills her entire body. It must be the weekend! Otherwise there's no way Ben would be up getting breakfast ready, especially given how late they'd gotten to bed last night. It must have been close to four o'clock by the time they'd come stumbling home from their favorite Italian place. This was after two bottles of rosé and way too many glasses of Ramazzotti, urged on them by Beppo in that charming way of his, just like he did every time they ate there. When they got to the stairs, Ben scooped Clara up in his arms and carried her to the third floor without batting an eye, simply because her feet were hurting from all the impromptu dancing on the way home.

Now he carefully sets the tray down and gingerly sits next to her. Tenderly his lips begin to brush against her face.

"Actually I had something else in mind," Ben whispers in her ear.

Clara is a little more awake now. She feels Ben's fine, short stubble on her chest. His mouth slides slowly down her paper-thin nightie.

She loves it when he wakes her up like this. Nothing gives her such a sense of being taken care of than to feel his strong body so close to hers.

But he's very light. And she can barely sense the familiar way he smells. Something is different today.

Hesitantly, as if in a trance, Clara opens her eyes. And all at once she's wide awake.

For a second she feels like a stranger, trapped in a time that's unfamiliar to her.

And suddenly it's back again, the brutal reality: Ben isn't here.

Ben will never be here again.

She must have been dreaming. It's been a long time since Clara had a dream. In the last two months and five days, she hasn't smiled either—though she's tried to, every now and then. Like for example when she's attempting to keep her mother from launching into another one of her exhausting pep talks. If she were the old Clara again, maybe her mother would be more willing to leave her alone and let her manage all by herself.

All by herself . . .

That's exactly how she's felt since that day in January when her beloved Ben fell to his death from a balcony.

All by herself. Abandoned. Alone. Alone with all the thoughts that haunt Clara like a giant shadowy figure. Especially at night. Again and again she'll wake from a restless, dreamless sleep. Only for a fleeting, peaceful second between sleep and waking does Clara feel like the Clara she used to be.

Before Ben died, Clara was a confident, independent woman. A woman who was less romantic and sentimental than most of her friends. It was this strong, rational side that Ben had found captivating about her right from the start. They each had different ways of looking at the world, true, but together their separate worldviews formed a wonderfully complete vision that was a source of comfort and support for both of them.

Whenever they fought, they were quick to make up afterward. One of them would say something, sheepishly, trying to swallow their pride, then a gesture here or there would give way to a familiar touch as their bodies drew closer. This was usually followed by a playful chase around their cozy one-bedroom apartment, until finally Clara fell exhausted into Ben's arms. As he held her she could feel his fingers on her ribs beneath her shirt, and all he would have to do then was feign like he was going to tickle her and already she would be shrieking with panic and delight. When finally he would lean in closer and tenderly kiss her slender neck just below her ear, whispering affectionate nonsense as he kissed her. At moments like this he would call her "Lilime" in a soft voice. Only Clara knew that this was short for *Lieblingsmensch*—favorite person. Her bright green eyes would begin to shine every time, and they would make love without another word.

Even after being together for more than three years, there was still such a feeling of closeness between them every time they made love that it was as if they had only just fallen for each other.

But not the night it happened. One reproach had led to another, and today Clara would do anything never to have uttered such harsh words.

She could still hear the sound of the door slamming when Ben left the apartment, beside himself with anger. It was the first and last time he'd ever left without saying where he was going.

When she thinks back on how relieved she had been that she was now by herself and was free to vent to her closest friend Katja about how immature and irresponsible Ben was, despite his thirty-two years . . . Clara can still feel the guilt coursing through her whole body like burning acid.

True, that night she had kept an eye on her cell phone the whole time she was talking to Katja on the landline, discussing whether she should teach Ben a lesson this time and take off for a whole night, something she'd normally never do. But no text came from Ben. And he was always texting her. Whenever he had a break between classes at the university, was out on the road with his band, or over at his buddy Carsten's place getting loaded—if for no other reason than that he didn't want to give Clara the chance to feel annoyed, he would considerately send a few reassuring words to "Lilime."

When they first met at Cheers, Clara had been skeptical. She'd heard all the rumors about Ben Runge the lothario, the guy who'd turned the head of every pretty girl in Lüneburg. But with his texts, Ben made an effort to show her that she was the only one he cared about. And so, whenever he thought of her, he would send her a text and make her phone light up for a brief moment, as a kind of token of his love.

But since that horrible night, Clara hadn't received a single text.

Ben doesn't contact her at all anymore.

He remains forever silent.

clara

Clara is nervous. Her compassionate leave is now officially over. Today is her first day back at work since Ben's death.

The doctor did offer to write her a note granting her an extra week off, but by this point, Clara longs for structure and everyday routine. She can no longer bear lying awake all night and staying in bed till late morning without really feeling rested. It makes her feel like a moldy, dried-up piece of bread. If, early on, her mother hadn't started making her take a short walk every afternoon, she probably still wouldn't have the nerve to even leave the apartment.

The first time she went out grocery shopping on her own to replenish her supply of canned soup, Clara had felt like everyone could see the pain written on her face. The cashier hadn't even been able to look her in the eye. And Clara had felt this indescribable urge to just shout out: "Yes, my boyfriend is dead, and nobody knows why!"

But there are a few things connecting her to the world outside that are more pleasant, that lend her strength, or at least that don't add to her sorrow. Niklas, her boss, for example, has called her every week to ask how she's doing and to assure her that where her job is concerned she has nothing to worry about. Her colleague Antje was taking care of everything, he'd tell her, but she could never take Clara's place as the best graphic designer at the agency.

Clara knows that Antje isn't very passionate about advertising anyway and doesn't understand how Clara can be so committed to her career. By this point, Clara also has to admit to herself that she spent far too many nights alone at the office instead of enjoying a relaxing night at home with Ben or going out with him and simply celebrating life. She had always wanted to do perfect work, to be able to present the client not with a single half-hearted mock-up but rather a brilliant design and two excellent alternatives on top of that. It gave her the most satisfying feeling when the client ended up choosing her favorite. Most of the time, though, Clara would just enjoy her success in silence, and her triumph was usually brief.

At heart I'm a loner, thinks Clara, *and when I'm working on my designs no one can bother me. It's like I'm in a trance; I can stay like that for hours.* But this trance-like state seems unattainable now—reality mercilessly blocks her way into this beautiful other world.

Clara hopes that work will do her good. After all, at the office she'll have to pull herself together, she can't just sit there brooding for hours at a time, wondering what was going on in Ben's head that night and how she was supposed to get by without him. She still hasn't found an answer. But if Clara goes even a few minutes without thinking about Ben and his death, guilt immediately takes hold of her again.

She'd gone for a walk with her grandmother Lisbeth in Lüneburg's Kurpark yesterday and had left abruptly because she absolutely had to hurry home to look at photos. She was worried that she might have forgotten Ben's face and wanted to recover the supposedly lost memories right away. When she finally got back home, with a stitch in her side from running the whole way, she grabbed all the photo albums off the shelf, frantically opened them, and lined up the nicest photos in a row on the floor.

Should she put a photo of Ben on her desk at the office? One that shows that clever smile of his, that preserves at least some small piece of his charm? How would her colleagues react? Today Clara will be seeing them for the first time since the funeral.

But she's tired of having this strange feeling like she's some kind of leper. She doesn't want to make things uncomfortable for the others unnecessarily.

The worst thing isn't the clumsy expressions of sympathy from friends and coworkers who are simply trying to offer their condolences. *Rather it's all the words that go unsaid*, thinks Clara—*they're what I find so humiliating.*

Like her mother's neighbor, who just leaped up and left the kitchen without a word when Clara stopped by her mother's house one day unannounced.

At least at the agency everybody knows that today is her first day back. Hopefully everything goes well, Clara prays as she pushes open the glass door of the office building in Lüneburg's industrial district. She's gotten here extra early; this way maybe she'll have a chance to acclimate herself to being back at the office before the day's work routine comes crashing down on her again.

She's incredibly nervous as she steps out of the elevator. The hallway seems ominously quiet. Not even Viola, the receptionist, is here yet.

Clara is surprised to see that the door to her office is closed. Is her brain already so addled at this point that she's gotten Sunday confused with Monday?

But Niklas's gaudy Fiat Spider convertible was parked right in front of the entrance, so her boss must be here at least. Since his door isn't open either, Clara decides to wait till later to say hello to him.

"Surprise!" Clara's office erupts into a many-voiced shout as she turns the handle and opens the door.

The whole team is standing in a semicircle around her desk and looking at her expectantly. Over her Mac hangs a banner with the words "Welcome Back!" And on her desk is a large glass vase with a bouquet of colorful spring flowers.

Before Clara can say anything, Niklas takes the floor.

"Looks like we managed to pull off this early-morning surprise. Hello, Clara!" He clears his throat and looks around awkwardly at everyone standing there. "Right, um, we're just happy to have you back. And since I've known you long enough by now to know that you don't like to be the center of attention, I won't make any big speech or anything. All I wanted to say was that we all wish you a warm welcome! So okay, and now let's get back to work, everybody."

The group gives a muted round of applause and quickly breaks up. Only Antje goes up to Clara and greets her with a quick hug. Clara is very touched. She has to fight back tears.

"Thanks," she whispers softly.

Hearing this, Antje looks at her wide-eyed and quickly responds: "Hey, what for?"

Clara shrugs her shoulders and smiles. It's her first smile in weeks.

sven

should've just stayed in bed! Sven regrets having to wake up so early as the garlic breath of the man standing across from him in the packed Landungsbrücken-bound tram car hits him in the face—no chance now of enjoying the coffee with almond syrup and foam he'd bought. As angry as he is at this fat man speaking loudly to a colleague and projecting his stench into the already foul air, he's angrier at himself. It's been at least ten weeks and he still hasn't managed to fix his road bike. There's really no excuse for it; whatever explanation he might come up with would be lacking. Too much alcohol and too many sordid hookups, not enough positive input, which in turn only slowed down what little inner drive he had left.

The strange thing is that Sven has always thought of himself as a pretty fortunate guy. Somehow, though, for the past three years, things just haven't been running quite as smoothly as they used to. True, his career as a business journalist is going fine, he's well respected in his field, but ultimately no one is impressed anymore by the fact that he regularly interviews all the big CEOs. Least of all himself. At editorial meetings he's constantly letting his mind wander instead of impressing the two editors in chief or his colleagues with razor-sharp comments or brilliant article ideas.

What happened to him?

When he first got to college to study economics, he was full of excitement and fresh ideas. He was politically active, had lots of friends, and worked out every day. He loved being out in the harbor air—early in the morning, when most of the residents of Altona were still zonked out in their beds.

Could his lethargy have something to do with the breakup with Fiona? Sven refuses to see a connection. If he did, then that would mean having to admit to himself that he was powerless in the face of his problems. He prefers to tell himself that she wasn't really his true love. But even though so much time has passed since then, he can still see the image clearly in his mind: Fiona pressed up against her Mini Cooper, her arms slung around another man's body.

Maybe it's partly his anger at himself that keeps him from closing that chapter once and for all. Instead he continues to torture himself with the question of why he didn't have the guts to fling his bike to one side, march up to the two of them, and take command. He should have shown that dickhead who Fiona was really with.

But maybe he had already screwed things up before then. Maybe Fiona had been right to criticize him all the time for never showing her how much she really meant to him. His coworker Hilke also tried to make him see that when Fiona finally moved out of the loft they shared, the mysterious other man wasn't the reason, just the catalyst.

Sven likes Hilke and trusts her, but he would never let her know this—not without a very compelling reason. For him, she's like the sister he never had. She's never let him down in all the years they've worked together. Hurt his feelings, sure, but never on purpose; really it's just that in her open and almost naive way she can't help but make blunt comments again and again. She hits him where it hurts. In all the time they've shared an office on the seventh floor, hardly a week has gone by without her saying something that makes him stop and think. She simply has a knack for always finding his sore spot.

"You're just in a bad mood because you're not getting any good sex anymore"—that was the latest salvo, launched across their desks just last Monday, when Sven was muttering obscenities and cursing about some emails. "If you spend next weekend wasting your precious time on earth on the internet again with that stupid guild of yours, I'll lose all affection for you!"

Sven could only smirk. Hilke had looked a bit sheepish after making such a bold comment. She knew she'd gone a bit too far this time. Not because she'd touched so pointedly his biggest weakness, the computer game *World of Warcraft*, but more because her words had hit so close to home. In response, Sven had cleared his throat and quickly muttered something about not having any time next Saturday anyway because he really had to go look in on his father again; it had been too long.

These visits were another reason why it would be wise to finally get the bike working again or at least take it to a shop if he couldn't do it himself, Sven now thinks. He does his best to hide behind his newspaper, but its contents hardly interest him.

Even though it's already quite mild for March, he's still wearing his old brown leather gloves so that he won't have to touch any of the train surfaces that have already been touched by a thousand other people before him. It turns his stomach, everyone squeezing up against one another like this, penned in tight between the doors. He decides to just throw away his lukewarm coffee as soon as he gets out.

Week after week, every Monday morning makes him more aware of how pathetic his life feels right now. A few minutes from now, when Hilke greets him cheerfully and asks how his weekend was, he'll have to make something up to draw attention away from the fact that, once again, he didn't manage to do anything he'd actually meant to do. He hadn't dealt with the busted gear shifter, he hadn't gone jogging, and he hadn't gone out to the bar for a beer with his friend Bernd. And he hadn't checked in with his father, either. He just doesn't know what the two of them can talk about.

Sven gets off the train and starts walking toward the magazine's offices. He takes several deep breaths, in and out, as if he could expel from his body all the air that the other commuters had emitted. *Something has to change*, Sven thinks. *I finally want to feel like I'm alive again.* But he has absolutely no idea how he's supposed to make this happen.

clara

Only that night, when she's lying in bed and reflecting on her first day back at work, does it slowly become clear to Clara that Niklas had done just the right thing that morning. The warm greeting had made it much easier to jump back into things than she had feared it would be in the days leading up to today. The thought of everyone stopping by her office one by one, with eyes lowered, had been just awful.

Suddenly Clara starts grinning in spite of herself. How many times had she tried—gently, to be sure—to alert her boss to the fact that he just didn't have a head for the creative side of things, that rather his one strength was going out and finding new clients. But today he'd had a really good idea for once.

Clara feels pleasantly exhausted from all the familiar and yet new impressions the day has left on her, and for the first time in a long time she looks forward to going to sleep. Still, though, she feels a real need to talk to someone. It's too late to call her grandmother. And if she were to call Katja they'd get into a long chatty conversation like they usually did.

She used to tell Ben everything. How much she would like to tell him about her day today. Today it had been evident that they really needed her at the agency. Just like that, tomorrow morning she would be taking part in a meeting to prepare for an important pitch. And that felt good; it felt a bit like normalcy.

Acting on an impulse, Clara suddenly grabs her cell phone, sits up, and with trembling fingers and pounding heart, she types a text message to Ben.

> My darling! Oh, where are you? How are you? I miss you every single second, but today I laughed again for the first time. Loving you forever, your Lilime

Clara takes a large sip of her nightly fruit tea, gives a satisfied nod, and hits Send.

sven

What a slap in the face!

Sven is still sitting like a stone before a printout of his article on the new study put out by the German Institute for Economic Research, which his editor in chief had dropped on his desk without saying a word—he'd just looked at him, eyebrows raised.

He's used to his articles sailing through without him having to make any major changes. Since he usually sticks to what was discussed at the editorial meeting, his approach to the subject matter usually gets the nod without him having to go through a second or third round of revisions. Apparently though he's going to have to start this piece all over again, completely rewrite it, even though it's well past time to go to press.

"Definitely an interesting take. But lacks focus! W.B." Thus read Walter Breiding's comments, scrawled on the last page after he'd drawn a diagonal line from top to bottom, slashing through all six manuscript pages.

This had never happened to Sven before! Not even during his internship at the *Hannoversche Allgemeine Zeitung*. Or at *News of the World* magazine in London. Before he can start letting loose about Breiding to Hilke, it becomes clear to him that what he wrote this time really is crap.

He'd put as little heart into the article as he had into the list that he'd begun last night at home over a bottle of red wine. Hilke had suggested that he write down his specific life goals for the coming years. She swears by this method. But Sven hadn't gotten too far before turning his attention back to his article.

And now he has to admit that, having failed to do enough research, he had simply shifted the focus of his article to serve his own arguments. And unfortunately he'd done this so blatantly that Breiding had no other choice but to throw the article back in his face.

"Let me guess," Hilke says, smirking, "he finds it a bit underseasoned?" Quoting one of Breiding's typical lines is her way of letting Sven know that she very much noticed the boss's appearance, despite having never looked up from her computer screen.

"Eh, no," Sven forces himself to reply. "I think it's more like the main course never arrived."

"Let me see!" Hilke scans the pages and says sympathetically: "Looks like a night shift to me. Do you need any help?"

"If I can't think of anything clever by midnight, I'll give you a call," Sven replies and lifts the right corner of his mouth into something resembling a grin.

"Oh yeah, I'm sure Martin would love that!" Hilke replies sarcastically.

"Don't worry. I wouldn't want to put any strain on your marriage."

"Oh, it takes more than that to strain a marriage," Hilke replies, not without a little pride.

"Yeah, and I really have to ask myself sometimes how you're still holding it together after so many years . . ." Sven is worried

that he might sound envious. But it's true he doesn't really understand.

"Love, that's the secret. L-O-V-E. But of course you don't know
anything about that!"

Even though he's sure Hilke doesn't mean it like that, Sven feels
a faint stab of pain. But he chooses not to say anything.

"If you need any last-minute help with matters of the heart or
anything else, feel free to call. Otherwise I'll see you tomorrow."

"Yeah, thanks. Have a good night."

. . .

It's already past midnight, and Sven is still sitting at his computer.
When the custodian stopped by a little while ago, he realized he
hadn't moved an inch since Hilke left. But she simply vacuumed
around him and emptied his wastebasket as quietly as possible.

Not a thing has happened on his computer screen. Sven just
feels zero motivation to start the piece over again. Instead he sits
in his chair with a view out the window of HafenCity. The rede-
velopment project on the harbor is still just a giant construction
site, though not uninteresting to look at. He stares and lets his
mind wander. He can feel an ominous twinge in the back of his
neck. There's a pain beginning to announce itself just above the
shoulder blades; it's bearable, for now, but still uncomfortably
present.

Outside it's dark, and his stern face is reflected in the windowpane. Sven asks himself if he actually likes what he sees. He feels
pretty good about his body, as out of shape as he might be currently. But he has no real opinion of his face. He feels it to be
average, neither particularly ugly nor particularly attractive. His

old girlfriends had liked his eyes best. They're his mother's. She apparently had the same pale blue eyes. She died when Sven was four years old, and he wonders sometimes what else he might have inherited from her.

Fiona had always said his eyes glowed like the icy-blue eyes of a husky, almost sinister-looking, but irresistibly handsome. She found his gaze sexy. He usually didn't let it show, but the compliment made him happy every time he heard it.

Catching sight of himself now, however, Sven feels he looks rather pallid, like he's staring into the face of a lifeless figure. His hair has grown thin. At forty-two, he feels old for the first time in his life. *Would a wife, to say nothing of a family, bring about any sort of change?* Sven wonders. But quickly he checks himself—he shouldn't start dwelling on any romantic fantasies. Sooner or later, one way or another, they would just lead to disappointment.

There hadn't been any kind of enduring love in his life up to this point. And there wouldn't ever be, either—on this point Sven is convinced. With Fiona, he had been able to imagine the two of them having a future together. But the day was bound to have come eventually when all the wonderful facets that together made up the feeling of being in love would have vanished, gone in a way that was as mysterious as it was irrevocable. People just aren't made to spend their whole lives with the same person. Even if corny movies and books never got tired of suggesting the opposite.

Just as Sven is deciding to put together that list of his life goals after all, his cell phone dings. He reaches in his bag to see who could be texting him this late. *No doubt it's Hilke*, Sven thinks, sending him a few words of encouragement before she gets into bed with her husband. Sven can sense himself envying her for her relationship.

But when he reads the text, it's immediately clear to him that the message isn't meant for him at all. Clearly some utterly hopeless romantic has got the wrong number. Sven gets the gist all the same: If you're in love, your brain turns to mush. If you're not in love, you go numb.

clara

A sign!"

"Huh?" Katja mumbles, slightly annoyed, on the other end of the line. "I'm totally lost here. Give me a second to wake up."

Clara has thrown on her old velour jacket and sat down on the windowsill in the kitchen, her legs pulled up so that her bare feet aren't touching the cold tile floor. She's still totally worked up and is afraid that Katja is either going to call an ambulance or just laugh at her.

"All right, one more time, babe. Start from the very beginning. Take a deep breath and then tell me again what happened, nice and slow, okay?"

"I mean the damn lights went out!" Clara says again and is startled by how hysterical her voice sounds. "I sent Ben a text, and as soon as the display said 'message sent' the damn lights went out in the bedroom!"

"You did what?"

"Nothing! I didn't do a thing. That's what's so crazy about it!"

"No, I mean, you sent Ben a text?!"

Clara has to swallow hard. She doesn't want to start bawling yet again. Not now, not after such a successful day. She tries to sound as calm as possible.

"Yeah, I know it's stupid. And it's not like I've ever done something so ridiculous before. Honest! But I just felt like doing it. And then, just like that, everything went dark!" Clara realizes that she's talking a bit too loudly again.

"Um, okay, so you sent the text, and then it got dark?" Katja asks, taken aback.

"Yes."

"And you're sure that you didn't turn the lights off yourself?"

"Katja, come on! I mean I know you all think I'm still out of my head, but I'm not an idiot!"

"Hmm, well, it does sound a bit spooky . . . ," Katja mumbles quietly, as if she's talking to herself.

"Yes, that's what I'm saying. I was totally freaked out and started flipping the light switch up and down like crazy. Then suddenly the lights came back on. So I mean the lamp still works totally fine."

"Well, okay, so I guess everything's all right then," Katja yawns into the receiver.

"Nothing is all right!" Clara's voice is so tearful now that Katja can barely understand her.

"Listen, babe, why don't you get all your stuff together for tomorrow and come spend the night at my place tonight? I'll pick you up, okay?"

"I don't think I can. I have to get going really early tomorrow."

"Mm-hmm, all right, then try to get some sleep now. Tuck yourself in nice and warm. And make yourself some hot chocolate beforehand—and don't forget the whipped cream! I'm sure you've gone all day again without eating anything but a bowl of soup!"

Clara lets out a sigh. Her grandmother is always preaching the exact same thing. Just yesterday, when she was at her grandparents' place for a visit, her grandmother had tried every trick in the book urging Clara to get some more "meat on her bones," as she lovingly puts it.

Clara used to fret about extra pounds. But by this point even she is beginning to worry a little about her loss of appetite.

Within just a few weeks after the wake the little love handles around her hips had just about vanished. Since Ben has been gone, Clara has to choke down even the smallest of meals, without taking any enjoyment in them. Sometimes on Saturdays she still drives out to a big supermarket to buy cans of soup and buttermilk. But she only does this because it makes her feel a little closer to Ben. He loved plunging into the big adventure that was grocery shopping on Saturday mornings. He was always coaxing Clara into coming along with him, usually by holding out the prospect of a family-sized box of stracciatella ice cream.

Ben just fundamentally did not care, at all, what other people thought about him. He could start juggling a handful of oranges in the middle of a crowded supermarket or get Clara to join him in a little dance routine by the freezer section. He had a theatrical way of planting a kiss on her in some unlikely place—her nose, her elbow, her knee—while they were standing in line or just brazenly pinching her butt so that she let out a shriek—it was anything but embarrassing to him. Wherever he went he was immediately the center of attention. True, there were times when Clara felt a bit mortified when she was with him, but most of the time she watched him with adoration.

And on the other hand, there was simply no one better than Ben when it came to making Clara feel that she was the most wonderful woman in the world. Even if he did like to overdo it with his compliments. Whenever she was complaining for the umpteenth time about her breasts being too small or her boring dirty blond hair, he had always been able to convince her that she was the only one, that everything revolved around her.

But then how could he ever have left her? If he was supposed to have loved her so much? Or did he not leave her at all? Was it all just the workings of ruthless fate?

Clara feels the despair rising within her. She quickly promises Katja that she'll snuggle down with another cup of fruit tea and hangs up.

Which is more distressing, really: the idea of a young life and a happy relationship being snuffed out forever by a tragic accident? Or the feeling that in reality you barely knew your own partner, the man with whom you shared every day of your life for more than three years? How long must Ben have been suffering?

All these painful questions keep popping up out of the blue, and Clara admonishes herself to put them out of her mind. It's time she started facing her new life, one step at a time. The last thing she wants is to continue to be a burden to her family and to Katja. And above all she wants to stop adding to Lisbeth and Willy's worries.

It's already bad enough that things are getting worse for her grandfather with every year, Clara thinks, running her hands down her face. And her grandmother? Ever since Willy's stroke she, too, had lost so much of her vitality and joy in life. Most of the time her grandfather doesn't do much else than sit in his arm-chair. He tries to hide behind his books on astronomy or history, but his eyes get tired very quickly.

Clara suddenly gets a lump in her throat when she thinks of yesterday's visit with her grandparents. Together they sat at the dining room table, which, just like Lisbeth and Willy, is well over seventy years old.

Her grandmother is such a dainty woman, Clara thought as she began slicing up the freshly baked cake. And yet even still she's robust and strong, and there's always been a warm radiance about her.

Clara is very close to her, even if she inherited neither her physical features nor any noticeable character traits. She takes more after her grandfather, who just like her father has intense, bright green eyes. Either way, generally speaking the relatives on her father's side of the family are really much closer to Clara's heart. Could that be because she lost her father so early?

She was just eleven when he was diagnosed with colon cancer. He died of it a short time later. It all went very fast, and sometimes Clara is ashamed of herself because she can only vaguely remember his voice, his face, or the way he smelled.

Her relationship with her mother has been strained ever since. It's so much easier for Clara to speak to Lisbeth about all the things weighing on her mind.

"So, my child. You get yourself a nice big dollop to top this with," her grandmother commanded and reached for the crystal dish with the whipped cream.

"But your cake tastes so delicious just like it is!" Clara replies, knowing full well that any objections on her part will be roundly ignored.

While she was still eating her cake and listening to the usual chitchat about the neighbors and the latest argument they were having—something to do with the introduction of paper recycling bins that were going to be managed by a private company—Willy got up and headed back to the living room.

"How's he doing these days?" asked Clara as she took another piece of cake.

"Well, you know, he's struggling along, for better or worse. He really misses riding his bike all the time like he used to." Usually Lisbeth would smile and change the subject, but this Sunday she lowered her gaze. "I'm afraid he's getting to the point where he doesn't want to go on anymore."

"How come?" Clara could feel her heart beating faster all of a sudden. "What happened?"

"Nothing's happened, nothing at all. But he's been saying so little recently. And for a long time now his sleep has been very restless."

"What do you mean, restless? Could he have had another stroke?"

"No, no, we would have noticed that. He's still going to the doctor regularly. I just think that he's . . ." Lisbeth had trouble finding the words. "I think that, emotionally, he's not doing so well."

"But Grandma, that's no wonder! Especially now, when it's getting to be spring and he can't do all the things he used to anymore."

"Well, sure. But I think it's even worse than that somehow."

"But what makes you think that?"

"I just sense it."

"Okay, but what exactly do you sense?"

"I can't explain it. He's just not doing very well."

Clara swallowed hard. She didn't dare probe any further, but she had the feeling her grandmother was keeping something from her.

"Oh, honey," sighed Lisbeth. "I know he might seem like a big grump sometimes, but he's very soft and sensitive at heart. It's just tearing him up inside that . . . um, well, you know, that so much has changed."

"You mean since Ben's been gone?" Clara asked softly, and hearing her own voice as she asked the question she knew there was no need for an answer.

She was stunned. It had never occurred to her that her grandfather might be suffering so much from this horrible turn of events.

"You know him. He always thinks way too much about things," Lisbeth added and started clearing the table.

Slowly it dawned on Clara. This might not be about Willy at all or at least not completely; maybe it was also about how Lisbeth no longer knew where to turn with her worries. Sure, she had a few old friends and a second son. But the son lived with his family near Frankfurt and rarely came to Lüneburg to visit.

Lisbeth came back to the table with a Tupperware container full of cake.

"But I thought . . . ," Clara began and hung her head—she couldn't bear looking at her grandmother's worried face.

Then Lisbeth reached for her granddaughter's hand and said: "Grandpa loves you so terribly much. Even if he doesn't say much, he knows that your sensitive little soul is hurt."

Even though Clara has firmly resolved never to be a source of worry for her grandmother again, tears still come to her eyes when she thinks back on the scene now. But at this moment, she isn't sure if she's weeping on account of Ben or her grandparents. She can't help but utterly give in to her despair and self-pity. Clara cries harder than she has in weeks. She feels both guilty and, at the same time, like she's been treated unfairly—as if life had betrayed her.

In moments like these, when all she can feel is sadness and emptiness, the thought sometimes occurs to Clara: Maybe she should just check out, take the same cowardly route that Ben might well have chosen. She would simply take pills and cry herself to sleep, and everything would finally be good again. But she knows that taking such a step would only bring more misery into the world, not less. Her conscience immediately makes itself heard.

What would her grandmother, grandfather, and mother do without her? And Katja and her childhood friend Bea would definitely never forgive her for not confiding in them. It might even be her fault if her grandfather completely lost the will to live afterward.

Ever since Ben's death, Clara feels like she's in a glass prison. Her family, her friends, her coworkers—she can see them, they're all gathered around her and are there for her anytime she needs them. But she can't reach them. Even when she speaks to them, hardly any of them understands what she's really trying to say. Instinctively she can tell that even the most compassionate people eventually get to the point where they're no longer capable of dealing with all the things she has to get off her chest again and again. She can feel the loneliness creeping into her; it's almost a physical sensation. And every additional thought of Ben only separates her even further from everything she used to hold so dear.

Only when she's lying in bed again does Clara slowly start to calm down. In this moment only a single thought brings her comfort: the thought of texting Ben again.

> I think about you all the time. Give me another sign if you're doing okay. But make it one that doesn't scare me so bad! Loving you always, your L.

Even though Clara feels very weird about it and is almost a little afraid, she decides to make a daily ritual out of this, to let it become a cherished habit. From now on, every day, she's going to send a text out into the beyond.

sven

The next day, with his eyebrows raised and his voice rising to a theatrical pitch that disavows all seriousness, Sven reads aloud the following:

> Hello, darling! Can you maybe do something for my grandpa from up there? Somehow we're all missing the laughter we once had—and I'm missing you especially bad today.
> Your Lilime

Sven is about to tack on another indignant laugh at the end to make it unmistakably clear to Hilke that he finds the contents of the text absolutely ridiculous. But he can't laugh, because Hilke's reaction throws him off.

"Well, that's just heartbreaking. It sounds like a poor sad child talking to God," Hilke says earnestly and without any trace of a grin. "Give it here!" she quickly adds in a tone of voice that comes close to an order.

Sven hands her his iPhone with extreme reluctance—after all, the device is brand new and still free of any scratches or finger-prints.

"And where are the other two?" she asks. "I want to read all of them—and I mean now!"

Now Sven really does have to laugh. At Hilke. She acts as though he had just told her about a surprise audience with the pope or Elvis Presley coming back to life.

"What?" she asks indignantly.

"Oh, nothing," Sven says and shakes his head, amused.

"Have you written back yet?"

"No way. Why?"

"Men!" Hilke rolls her eyes and raises one eyebrow. "Well, for one thing you could at least let whoever this is know that they're going to all this trouble for nothing. After all, this Lilime person has no way of knowing that all their texts are going to the wrong number!"

All of a sudden Sven isn't so sure of himself.

But Hilke goes on, unmoved: "In fact, the texts are going to a cold, emotionless monster who is hateful to boot and has no sympathy for a poor little child. A child who is clearly very worried about their sick grandpa!"

And suddenly Sven actually does feel guilty. He asks himself if he really is such a dirtbag, one of these guys who only ever thinks about technology and tits.

Angrily he brushes the thought aside and fires back: "Okay, so first of all, a child would never address somebody as 'darling' or prattle on in such a corny way. And second of all, in the highly unlikely event that it really is some emotionally disturbed child, it would most certainly be more valuable from a pedagogical standpoint not to rob the kid of every illusion that there is a God or some other kind of heavenly figure out there. So you could also say I'm doing the kid a favor!"

Hilke's telephone rings and she throws Sven a stinging look across the desk before picking up.

Sven smiles his smug victor's smile and turns back to his piece on white-collar crime and insider trading at the stock market.

But still his thoughts keep coming back to this strange business with the text messages. Maybe he should try to write a crime novel about it one day.

He lets his imagination run wild as he continues to stare at his computer screen with a look of concentration on his face—this way Hilke can't interrupt him with one of her biting comments.

The crime novel would be about a murder in the snobby milieu of HafenCity. Some kind of insurance fraud with millions paid out in bribes. An employee catches wind of it and starts black-mailing the crooked boss at the head of the scheme. Then when another guy finds out about it, he ends up strangling the black-mailer in the heat of the moment in an underground parking garage and has to throw his body in the Elbe, not realizing that he was seen by a nine-year-old boy. But the boy is so afraid that he won't tell anyone. He doesn't know what to do about what he's seen, so he looks in the phone book for the number of a private detective. Fearing that a phone call or a handwritten letter could be more easily traced back to him, the boy decides to inform the detective about the murderer by text. He steals a neighbor's cell phone and uses it to send a text that puts the investigators on the right track and leads to the solving of the case . . .

Sven can't help but grin all of a sudden at what seems to him a really original idea.

Hilke must have been watching him closely; she immediately

lets fly with one of her obligatory comments: "Well, well, have you just discovered your sensitive side?"

"Cute."

"Yeah, it would really be too funny if it turned out that even you had a heart, my dear Svenny."

"Don't call me Svenny!" Sven fires back with indignation.

"Whatever you say, Svenny."

Now both of them have to laugh. Sven finally gives up and asks his colleague if she wants to join him for lunch.

clara

After her first week back at work, Clara is looking forward to having two days off. Still, she doesn't really know what to do with her time. Other than meeting up for coffee with Ben's sister, Dorothea, on Sunday, she has frighteningly little planned. Katja is off on another of her trips to who knows where. Sometimes Clara envies her for the independence her career as an interior designer gives her and for not having any set times when she has to be in a sterile office. It's true that oftentimes her friend has to work late into the night, especially when clients come up with spontaneous ideas that require her to throw out all her original plans. But Katja never complains. She seems to have really found her calling. Usually her work is even more important to her than the men in her life, who never stick around too long anyway.

Katja is always urging Clara to look for a new job as fast as she can. She says Clara is letting herself be taken advantage of and is extremely underpaid.

And in fact last summer there was a time when things really weren't looking too good for the agency. After an important client had bailed, Niklas had had to let four people go, two of them from the graphic design department. As a result, Clara had to put in an inhuman amount of overtime and for a monthly salary that was equivalent to what Katja makes in a single week.

But Clara feels a sense of responsibility for the agency's fortunes, especially in bad times. She likes Niklas and most of her coworkers, too. And anyway it's not like there are a ton of advertising agencies in this small city, which means she would be forced to find a job elsewhere. But driving the thirty miles to Hamburg every day and having to deal with all that crazy traffic? How often had she argued about this with Ben?

Generally speaking they had always gotten along very well. Most of the time they spent together, things were relaxed and harmonious. But as soon as a subject like money or responsibility came up, it was like someone had flipped a switch, and all of a sudden they were at each other's throats.

Of course Ben and Katja had good arguments when it came to Clara's advancing in her career. But Ben sure was one to talk, Clara would think at such moments. He paid just a measly portion of their rent each month, and other than that he tended to just live from hand to mouth.

If Clara ever were to quit her job, it would only be because she'd found a solid alternative. And another thing to consider: A position in Hamburg would also bring with it additional costs for the commute.

But the two of them didn't want to hear such small-minded arguments. Instead, Ben and Katja would insinuate that Clara simply enjoyed being number one at the agency, she enjoyed being indispensable, and she enjoyed letting herself be blatantly exploited.

After these conversations, Clara usually felt very lonely and misunderstood, above all by Ben. The way she saw it, he seemed incapable of even beginning to see the problems in their larger context. The plain truth was that from the very beginning she had had to take on the role of the sensible one in the relationship.

When they decided to move in together and went looking for an apartment, it was only because Clara had taken the initiative. Ben was staying over at her studio apartment most of the time, and she was tired of feeling crowded. He had moved out of the house after his parents' divorce, back when he was still in high school, and since then had lived in a string of different apartments with different roommates. Marijuana, alcohol, and even harder drugs were almost an everyday thing for him. Clara had never really wanted to know anything about all that. Finally they had reached an agreement that he could continue partying and amusing himself with what Clara thought of as his sketchy friends—but only two nights a week at the most.

This arrangement worked astonishingly well for the first two years. Sure, they still fought about it every now and then. She would accuse Ben of being selfish and hedonistic, and he would accuse Clara of being, as he put it, uptight. But on the other hand his exuberant attitude toward life could be infectious, and he was fairly good at freeing Clara from her tight corset at least every now and then, for example by stopping by on her lunch break and taking her out for a surprise picnic.

But before her last birthday, things had come to a head and they'd had a big fight. Clara wanted to go away somewhere for her thirtieth birthday so that she wouldn't have to deal with any silly idea of her mother's, like an over-the-top dinner or something like that. She wanted more than anything to just get out of town for a few days. But when, after several exhausting attempts to win him over to her plan, Ben made it clear to her that he just couldn't afford a trip, she gave up the idea. She'd countered by saying that she would of course pay for it all, but Ben wouldn't even hear of it. He was too proud to let Clara support him over and above their day-to-day expenses. Just like he was too proud to accept financial support from his parents.

And yet he had a knack for coming up with unconventional ideas to cheer Clara up. And in the end Ben had turned this birthday into something really special.

When she got home from work the night before her birthday, Ben intercepted her at the door, handed her a packed travel bag, and told her to get in the car. He blindfolded her with a handkerchief, cranked the volume all the way up on the Wir sind Helden CD, and drove her around the neighborhood for half an hour before he told her she could get out. Then he picked her up, carried her up a few stairs, took her shoes off, and set her down barefoot in warm, fine-grained sand. That this sand didn't come from any beach on the Baltic or any other nice vacation spot, Clara actually only realized when she was allowed to take the blindfold off. She was standing in the middle of their living room, where Ben had laid out a tarp and covered it in sand from the hardware store. Before it hit her that Ben had brought the vacation home just for her, his bandmates Knut and Michi started playing their acoustic guitars. Ben had written a song specially for Clara to celebrate her on her birthday. Taking inspiration from Ben and Clara's favorite album *The Dark Side of the Moon* by Pink Floyd, the song was about longing.

> *Whenever I see the moon*
> *I wish to come back as soon*
> *As possible to kiss your lovely smile*

Being with you a very sweet while,
Clara, my heart; Clara, my light,
Your beauty is shining bright—all over the moon.

Of course Clara thought the refrain was incredibly corny, but the gesture behind it, and the thunderous applause that suddenly came from the surprise guests in the kitchen, sent a pleasant tingling feeling down her spine, and still does, even today. It was such a wonderful party, the kind anyone would wish for on their birthday. Even Bea, who was so reserved, admitted that she envied Clara for having a boyfriend who was such a cool singer and always came up with such great ideas.

Looking back on that night, Clara can't help but start laughing and crying all at once. She knows that the pain will get a little easier to bear with every month. But will she ever understand Ben? How could she feel so close to someone who clearly never really opened himself up to her? Was that why Ben had so often escaped into drugs and music? Had she simply not realized at the time how low an opinion Ben had of his talent and himself? Was he plagued by guilt for playing the role of the artist and bohemian when in reality he felt like a failure?

That at least is what Carsten told her after it happened.

Clara starts to feel a mixture of fear and rage whenever she thinks of Carsten. Of course she actually really likes Ben's best friend, and she knows that he's a good guy at heart. But the plain truth was that the bond between the two men had always been a thorn in her side.

Ben had whiled away more time with Carsten than with any of his other friends. And he had spent more nights blitzed on drugs with Carsten than with anyone else, too. The last night of his life was no different. And yet at the crucial moment, Carsten hadn't been there. Apparently he'd gotten sick. At least that's what he'd told the police later on. Sick from too much alcohol and too many joints.

He must have been off in the bathroom for half an hour while Ben stayed outside on the balcony. No one knows if Ben got cocky from all the alcohol in his blood and recklessly sat down on the concrete railing—or if, after the horrible fight with Clara, he took this opportunity to end his own life.

Carsten, at any rate, didn't think Ben's deadly fall from the fifth floor was an accident.

In the first few days following Ben's death, Clara had categorically refused to accept the possibility that it could have been suicide. Night after night she would replay scenes from her memory of her life with Ben, but the puzzle pieces just wouldn't fit together.

Only after countless grueling conversations with Dr. Ferdinand, her psychologist, did Clara get the courage to gradually start venturing inside Ben's world. Little by little, she began to understand that Ben might possibly have suffered from a personality disorder and could very well have repressed it or kept it secret for years. But even if at every session Clara learned more and more about the different pathological indicators and tried to fit Ben's life into this pattern, in the end what remained was only the sobering knowledge that there was absolutely no comfort to be found in his death.

Her Ben, a young man with dreams and hopes, with talents and faults, had died much too soon and for no reason at all. He hadn't left a suicide note. All that remained for Clara, his family, and his friends were memories, photographs, and his songs.

For the first time in a long time, Clara now dares to go over to her desk to get the burned CD with the song on it that Ben had given to her on her birthday. With trembling hands she reaches for the jewel case, which she'd illustrated with chalk markers that same night. A moon in silvery, shimmering hues, shining brightly out into the dark universe.

But when she opens the case, she gets a massive shock. On the back of the booklet a few lines are written, in handwriting that is more than familiar to her:

For Lilime, my great little artist! Ben

sven

Sven lies on his couch, his hands behind his head, and stares at the ceiling. It's Saturday night. There's some kind of reality show playing on television that doesn't actually interest him.

He's waiting for another one of these mysterious texts. By this point, he's spending more time thinking about these brief messages than he'd care to admit. He keeps puzzling over who they could be coming from and whether he might not be the intended recipient after all. Who knows, maybe it's someone he knows trying to mess with him. An old coworker, maybe, or someone from his Tai Chi club, whose meetings he hasn't gone to for months now.

Weirdly enough, the mysterious sender wrote a text last night with the words *Thank you for your message*. Maybe the texts actually were reaching the person they were intended for but were also being sent to him as the result of a technical glitch, like he was cc'd or something.

Sven decides to do some research when he gets to the office on Monday morning to find out if something like that is theoretically possible—and above all, if there isn't some way of learning the identity of the sender, even though they clearly want to remain anonymous and their number isn't listed anywhere.

Of course, Sven could also just call the number and politely ask the person to stop texting him. But somehow he just wouldn't feel right doing it. Maybe he's just curious, simple as that.

Really, though, Sven considers himself a discreet person. He doesn't get involved in things that don't concern him. It's different of course with research that he has to do for professional reasons. *Every person probably has some part of themselves that's eager to find out secret information*, Sven thinks as he pours himself some more wine. *But that doesn't make everybody a journalist.*

At the end of the day he's proud that he gets to work for an internationally recognized magazine and be part of a respected news organization. And things have gone a fair amount better for him over the past week than they had been going for most of the last few months. Even Breiding, in stark contrast to his usual arrogant manner, had praised his interview with the new Special Adviser on Sport and Development at the United Nations.

After a few glasses of red wine, a gift from his father, Sven sees that it's now half past ten. He reaches for his phone again. He's surprised that he hasn't gotten a text yet today. He double-checks the display to make sure. Nothing. Disappointed almost, he gets up and heads to the bathroom.

Just as he's reaching for his toothbrush, the *ding* goes off to signal that a text has come in. He immediately sets the toothbrush down again and hurries over to his phone. He saved the unknown sender in his contacts as "No Name." No Name writes:

> Finally started painting again today—for you only: Dark Side of the Moon! In love and gratitude, xoxo, your Lilime

Suddenly Sven has to grin a little in spite of himself. The Pink Floyd record is one of the oldest in his collection. He walks over to the long white shelf in the living room where he keeps all his LPs and CDs arranged in alphabetical order. He reaches up, pulls the record off the shelf, and looks at the cover, amused—it seems so familiar to him and immediately brings back memories from his teenage years. The first parties, wood-paneled basement rooms; his buddies from back then; his first love . . . He was with Michaela for more than two years. Sven looks back fondly on their time together, even though she never wanted to go all the way. Once his father had caught him clumsily trying to undo Michaela's bra after school. That was the most embarrassing experience in his life up to that point. He is far older today than his father was at the time, though he seemed much older to Sven back then.

Sven studies the record closely from every angle. Maybe he would feel more mature if his mother hadn't died so young? An expert would certainly be able to confirm this bit of amateur psychoanalysis.

But I've gotten along just fine in my life so far without professional help, thinks Sven—*even if Hilke likes to tell me otherwise.*

He puts the record on. It's been years since he last used his record player; it stands in such stark visual contrast to his B&O sound system with its top-of-the-line tube amplifiers. Curious to see whether it still works, Sven moves the needle to the fourth song, "Time." Immediately the music starts playing and the sound quality is amazingly good. Sven turns the volume up a little, pours the last bit of wine left in the bottle into his glass, and takes a hefty sip. He opens the door to the roof terrace and breathes in the cool air. His gaze sweeps over the buildings across the street.

Only a few lights are still on in the windows. But the moon is uncommonly bright, shining high above the city.

Life can be so beautiful, Sven thinks suddenly. And without really thinking of anything in particular, he tries to remember the last time he felt so good.

clara

Clara looks proudly at the painting on her easel. She's standing in the middle of the large kitchen, where it looks like she's just hosted a kindergarten art class. There are paints, brushes, and little glass jars everywhere.

Exhausted, she flops down onto a chair and only now realizes how numb her arms feel after painting for so long. She can't remember the last time she devoted herself to something with so much calm and purpose of mind. Sure, every now and then at the agency she had to do small drawings or sketch rough designs by hand. But a real oil painting and on such a large, framed canvas— it must be more than two years since she last managed to complete something on this scale. Clara has no idea why she stopped for so long. It does her good to escape into this fascinating world of color and form. A place where there are no gloomy thoughts and time and space are completely forgotten.

Over the last few months with Ben, she had simply never managed to make time for it. First she had wanted to fix up the new apartment and had been busy with redecorating work for weeks. There was no time left for picking up her brushes and being creative. And then, after that, she didn't have the space or the time anymore for things that she'd enjoyed doing when she was single. All she had was a stack of over a hundred drawings, watercolors, oil paintings, and etchings in the new basement storage space that she never so much as looked at.

Clara gets up to grab a soda from the refrigerator and is just sitting down again when suddenly her cell goes off. For a second, she hesitates to go out into the hallway to see who could be texting her so late. She can't help smiling when she catches herself thinking that Ben might have sent a message. But the text can't be from Ben; it can only be from Katja.

Clara drags herself to her feet and goes to get her phone. Sure enough, her friend asks:

Still awake? 😊

Clara hits the green button to call right back.

"Hey there, stranger, where are you?"

"On my way to your place, if that's okay?"

"Sure! But I thought you were still off somewhere way down south?"

"All right, so first of all, Kassel isn't exactly Bavaria, and second of all, it was a total bust. But I'll tell you all about it in a second."

"Okay. I'll go ahead and open a bottle of prosecco."

"And a box of tissues, please. Be right there!"

Before Clara can ask what Katja meant, her friend has already hung up.

Clara puts the painting in the closet, easel and all, hurries into the bathroom, tosses her old paint-spattered smock into the bathtub, and washes her hands, first with mineral spirits and then with lots of soap. When she catches sight of herself in the mirror, she can't help but give herself a big grin, almost like she's happy. She's just so pleased to have had a successful day, and now her friend is dropping by unexpectedly on top of that.

The buzzer for the door downstairs is already ringing when she heads back to the kitchen.

"Hey, babe!" pants Katja after a quick sprint up the stairs. She gives Clara a hug—as always, the embrace is a touch too rushed. Katja is an impulsive person through and through, and before Clara knows it, she's already parked herself on the couch.

"I have to confess something to you. But you can't get mad, okay?" Katja calls out toward the kitchen, where Clara is getting the prosecco, two glasses, and an open bag of chips.

"You've got me on the edge of my seat over here."

"So, confession number one: I wasn't in Kassel on business. Confession number two: I'm in love. Confession number three: The son of a bitch is married!"

Clara is so stunned she almost drops the bottle. Before she can say anything, Katja is already talking again: "I didn't tell you about it earlier because I . . . well, because I didn't know if you could hear it without getting sad."

"What can't I hear?" Clara asks with a little resentment in her voice.

"Just that I'm so happy because I met Robert. Check that, *was* happy!"

"Okay, so one thing at a time now. First off, you of all people should know that you can talk to me about anything. I still live on this planet; I'm not some alien who can't bear to listen to other people anymore."

"Yeah, sure. But—"

"And also," Clara interrupts her friend, her voice becoming a little gentler now, "I'm actually glad to hear that things are going well at least in some parts of the world."

"Well, they're not going quite as well anymore," says Katja in an unusually serious tone and drains her glass in a single gulp.

"All right, fire away. Start from the beginning. And don't you dare spare any details!"

It takes Katja more than half an hour to get everything off her chest. She's so worked up it's as if they hadn't spoken in months. She has kept this secret from her best friend for far too long, and meanwhile it's been totally consuming her. This thing with Robert had been totally casual at first, just like with all the other guys—after a brief, hot phase, Katja usually sends them packing; they get to be too demanding. Only once had Katja really been in love. At seventeen, she had fallen for a teacher who was much older—too old. And now she's finally caught the bug again. Clara can barely follow what she's saying; there are so many details and they all seem to be of vital importance.

Robert is six foot one and according to Katja fairly skeletal. He doesn't have a single ounce of body fat, works out almost incessantly, and spends the rest of his time in the office, working in investments or something like that. That is, when he's not spending time with his wife, who he'd neglected to mention until just five hours ago.

Katja is almost bursting with anger. And by the time Clara has opened a second bottle of prosecco, she's really letting loose.

"He's actually married. That asshole!"

Apparently his wife was just as unwitting as Katja was. Supposedly she had gone to visit her parents in East Frisia over the weekend, and Robert figured this was a great opportunity to invite Katja to their house. Up until that point they had only ever met at Katja's place in Lüneburg or in hotels in Hamburg—so long as he could declare the trip a business expense.

"You should have seen that asshole showing off that dump of his, blabbering on about how I should jazz it up and all that. Like what does the guy think, I'm going to conjure up a palace for him?" Katja is slurring her speech a little by this point, and her voice is reaching unexpectedly high pitches.

Clara isn't sure if the angry part is just now getting started or if the first tears are about to fall. Somewhat overwhelmed with the whole situation, she decides to stick to listening for now and wait to see if the "asshole" is still such an asshole in the morning.

Katja sighs and looks at Clara, bleary-eyed. "And speaking of goddamn assholes—how come you look so goddamn thin? I'm really starting to worry about you. Three months ago this bag of chips wouldn't have lasted an hour in this apartment!" She grabs a handful and gleefully stuffs them all into her mouth. Then suddenly she makes a face.

"Yuck, how old are these?"

"Oh, about three months . . ." Clara lowers her gaze and then adds with a slightly pained smile: "You know how it is. I'm on the hope-free diet."

Katja almost chokes. She gives Clara an uncertain look, hesitates for a moment, and then bursts out laughing, spraying huge quantities of half-chewed potato chips all over the couch in zero seconds flat.

"The hope-free diet!" she coughs. "Oh my God! The new weight-loss craze—developed by the two most pathetic losers in the universe: Clara Sommerfeld and Katja Albers. The recipe for weight-loss success: First fall in love, then separate—and just like that, you'll lose twenty pounds in ten weeks!" Katja is almost

screaming. Her laughter is so infectious that Clara can't help joining in and laughing with her until her stomach hurts.

"Okay, but for real now," Katja says finally and reaches for the
chips again. "We've really got to fatten you up!"

"Oh, cut it out. And now it's your turn again," Clara replies and
refills both of their glasses.

"Oh, I'm just going to let him sweat a bit. That always does the
trick."

"Well, in any case, you were definitely right not to let him get
away with that cowardly trick he tried to pull."

"Agreed. We can't let that kind of thing go unpunished!"

"Just don't end up punishing yourself worst of all. Do you really
think he's going to leave her?"

"No idea. But what we had going before now was really amazing. You should get online and find something for yourself!"

"Oh, sure. I'll put up a personal ad. Dried-up widow seeks
something male from the discard pile."

"Don't be ridiculous. Most couples meet online these days. It's
not just perverts or people who don't have any other options."

"Though there are plenty of married scumbags who lead a double life!"

"Ugh, tell me about it. And of all people, I had to fall for it!"
Katja hangs her head and lets out a big yawn. "But it's not like I'm
any better. How many guys have I led on by this point? There's
probably some nasty old angel up there who thought he'd even
the scales . . ."

Suddenly it's quiet in the living room. Katja gives Clara a bit of
a shamefaced look, like she'd eaten the last piece of cake that her
friend had been saving.

"And what was the avenging angel thinking in my case? What

did I ever do wrong?" Clara asks, more to herself than anything. Her words have a bitter aftertaste.

"Ugh, babe, I know, here I am griping about my banal relationship problems. But the burden you have to bear is so much heavier."

"Don't worry about it. Besides, if your burden feels as heavy as mine, we'll just have to lug both of ours together somehow. Maybe you really belong together, you and Robert, who knows?"

"Pssh, yeah, but only if he grows an ass to fill those pants of his—" Katja bursts out laughing again. When she's calmed back down she points to all the glasses and brushes lined up on the windowsill. "Hey, so what's all this stuff, anyway? Are you painting again?"

"Yeah, I started a large canvas yesterday," Clara replies with a grin that's a bit sheepish but still proud. "But I'm only going to show it to you when it's finished!"

. . .

The next day Clara is standing nervously at the door of Ben's sister's house. All week long she tried not to think about their coffee date. But she definitely didn't want to cancel on Dorothea. Clara feels responsible for Theo, as Ben always affectionately called his sister, and worries about how she's doing. She knows only too well that in the two months since Ben's death Dorothea still hasn't been able to come to terms with it. Nevertheless, even though she's just twenty-five years old, she has come an astonishingly long way, and for Clara's sake she's trying very hard to be brave.

They've agreed to find something nice to do, and because the weather is so pleasant this Sunday, Clara considers proposing to

Dorothea that they take a spring outing into Hamburg. If nothing else it's a way to ensure that they can breathe a little easier, without being reminded of Ben everywhere they go.

Sometimes Lüneburg seems like a deadly minefield. At their go-to bar, at Beppo's restaurant, at the movie theater, in the salt air and seclusion of the Kurpark, at the thermal baths, in the shops, and even on the most far-flung paths in the large idyllic city park . . . everywhere memories lie in wait. Like snipers lying in ambush, they fire little darts from their hiding places with pinpoint accuracy. Darts that pierce her straight through to the heart and hurt so much sometimes that Clara feels like the wind's been knocked out of her. At such moments she wishes she could just teleport into another time, like maybe five years into the future. Then hopefully everything will feel somewhat more "normal," even if nothing can ever be good again and a "normal" without Ben is actually unthinkable.

Maybe Katja's right. Maybe she should try to get her mind off things by seeing other men. Who can guarantee her anyway that she and Ben would actually have gotten married like they'd promised each other they would? If he really did take his own life, then that would mean he just left her, without even saying goodbye. But the Ben she knew and loved would never have done such a thing.

Clara can still vividly remember a show she saw on television one night about a year ago about people who just took off and left home in secret without saying goodbye. They leave their family and friends behind and start a new life somewhere else, usually abroad, and the people they leave behind become sick with worry because they don't know what happened. One mother they interviewed, whose son had vanished one day out of the blue, said that the uncertainty was much worse than the actual grief you felt for the person you loved and seemed to have lost. Hoping every day for their return, going over things from the past again and again in your mind searching for clues that could confirm or even explain their disappearance—it was sheer torture.

As Clara stands there frozen outside the house where Dorothea lives with her father, it suddenly hits her how thankful she can be that she and everyone else had the opportunity to say goodbye to Ben with dignity.

Clara wouldn't even say that the day of the funeral was the worst day of her life. There was an endless crowd of people present for the service and for the wake that followed it. And even though the mood was mostly set by Ben's music, which Katja and Knut from the band had helped her pick out, Clara didn't spend much time by herself or dwelling on lonely thoughts of Ben. Inside she had felt entirely calm, which her mother of course chalked up to her twin panaceas, Reiki massage and homeopathic pills. At the time Clara couldn't have cared less what was given to her. A sedative injection from the paramedic after the police had shown up at her door, broken the terrible news, and started asking questions, like was there a suicide note and what had Ben's living circumstances been like. After that sleeping pills every night and Bach flower drops and, sure enough, a few Reiki sessions with her mother, who thought that she could combat her deep emotional pain with the mere laying on of hands.

Really though Clara hates it when her mother comes at her with all that New Age nonsense. How many times have they butted heads over it! Her mother is an office manager, but for years she's been trying to find her true purpose in healing people. *The thing is*, thinks Clara, *if she wants to help people she should start by helping herself, as loopy as she is.* Her mother is always dragging her into these long conversations about being one with the energy or the universe or whatever else. Clara gave up trying to follow her a long time ago. Of course she loves her mother. But it's very different from the love she feels for her grandparents or even her father.

She and her mother are just fundamentally different. Karin is temperamental and brash. Clara meanwhile considers herself to be more quiet and introverted. Karin always has an opinion, which she's happy to share whether you ask her or not, while Clara prefers to hold back, which more than once has led her mother to criticize her for being calculating and unspontaneous. Even superficial things, like the way Karin dresses or how her apartment is decorated, seem so foreign to Clara sometimes that she asks herself from time to time whether she might actually have been adopted.

On the other hand, Clara is of course aware of how grateful she should be that her mother is so concerned about her. After all, not all of her well-meaning advice is completely off base. And when it came to everything that had to be taken care of before the funeral, Karin, and of course Katja as well, were one hundred percent there for her. Ben's parents, by contrast, weren't capable of pulling themselves together and throwing themselves into the job of tackling the practical side of things, like many grieving family members do out of desperation. No, it was Karin who took care of everything and bravely volunteered to sort through Ben's clothes—even though there were precious few of them that Clara was willing to part with.

Only Clara's clothes are to be found now in the dresser they used to share. Nevertheless, she has a few bags of his clothes in the closet and a few personal things sitting unsorted in boxes in the living room. These "urns" suggest a closeness that may never have existed and give Clara a vague sense of unease.

But day and night she wears the ring Ben gave her when he proposed, even though she really doesn't feel like the jewelry-wearing type. She did give Ben a ring for Christmas one year, though. It was one of a few cherished possessions that she placed in the grave with him. Which wasn't exactly legal.

About a month after the funeral, Katja had summoned all her nerve and convinced Clara to go along with this crazy idea. After all the turmoil surrounding the funeral, Clara had realized that she really would have liked to have given Ben something to take with him. And so, late one night, with hearts pounding like wild the whole time, the two of them actually went to the graveyard. In the dark, they dug a hole about a foot deep right in front of the newly placed headstone and laid a box down in it. In the box were a long farewell letter that Clara had written on the advice of Dr. Ferdinand, plus of course the ring, which the funeral home had handed her in a white envelope along with Ben's watch, his wallet, and his cell phone. Clara had put the phone into the grave as well, because it represented so many small tokens of his love and also the connection between them.

Clara had kept Ben's wristwatch for Dorothea. *Maybe today there will be a good opportunity to give it to her,* she thinks, then rings the doorbell. The few times they'd seen each other before now had been sad enough, Clara hadn't wanted to bring on any more tears with such a significant gesture.

Now she senses a vague feeling of dread when she hears footsteps inside. She really hopes that Ben's father isn't home. She prays that she's spared having to see him. He acts friendly enough, but there's always a look of reproach in his eyes when he asks how things are going with her. As if she'd be capable of just chatting away like she was at some old ladies' tea party.

"Hello!" Dorothea says cheerfully when she opens the door.

"I'm so glad we're doing this." Her voice seems very honest and heartfelt. She gives Clara a warm hug and Clara's fear quickly gives way to joy at seeing her again.

"Me, too! And if it's all right with you I figured we could head out right away. What do you think about driving to Hamburg? We could go for a walk on the Alster or on the Elbe," Clara says, keeping her voice down a little.

Dorothea nods eagerly and grabs her jacket.

Without another word they walk over to Clara's old Peugeot. Clara notices Dorothea glancing uneasily back at the house. Is she keeping an eye out for her father? Clara knows that he hasn't been managing well on his own since the death of his son. But it seems like Dorothea didn't tell him about her plans to meet up with Clara today.

When they're sitting in the car, Ben's sister says suddenly: "He's been drinking like a fish. I can't take much more of it!"

Clara is surprised; Dorothea isn't usually so direct. "Your father?" she asks.

"Yeah, I have no idea what to do. And even if I did, I'm probably not the right one to get him straightened out."

"Do you think he'd agree to get help somewhere?"

"Never. He's just as pigheaded as Benny," Dorothea says bluntly. It sounds bitter but affectionate nonetheless.

They don't say anything for a while, and somehow this, too, is a comfort to Clara. She's always felt close to Dorothea, but before now they hadn't had much of an opportunity to become something like real friends. This didn't have anything to do with the age difference between them; it was solely because Clara didn't want to intrude on their family business and usually sent Ben to see his sister on his own since the two of them rarely got to see each other anyway.

When after about thirty minutes of driving they cross the bridge over the Elbe, Clara suddenly feels a sharp pain in her chest. The last time she went to Hamburg was with Ben. They'd gone to a housewarming party for Lilo and Jan, a couple who used to live next door to them until they decided to move to Altona—they didn't want to waste away in the sticks, they said. The four of them usually had a lot of fun together though. There were countless nights when they'd gotten together at short notice to grill out, watch a movie, or play board games.

Clara realizes that she's close to losing herself in her thoughts, even though Dorothea is talking again now and saying how hard it's been with her divorced parents, who even after Ben's death haven't had much to say to each other and definitely not anything nice. She's afraid they might actually hate each other even more now, that each blames the other for what happened to their son.

"You know, maybe it's really all my fault," says Clara suddenly and bites her lip—she didn't actually want to put that on Dorothea right now.

"Are you crazy? You can't ever think like that, Clara!" Dorothea replies so quickly that it seems to come right from the heart. "Where did you come up with something so ridiculous?"

"I mean, it could be. If he really . . ." Clara hesitates. "If he really did decide to . . . to leave, then there would have been reasons for it. Maybe it was all too much for him, there was too much pressure, or what do I know . . ."

Clara can't look Dorothea in the eye. She stares doggedly at the red light on Rödingsmarkt. She's afraid that now that she's voiced her fears aloud for the first time, they'll turn out to be justified.

"What kind of pressure do you mean?"

"I mean, I don't know. I clearly forced him into a life that maybe he didn't even want. I did want it, all of it: a home, a family, a regular income. But maybe Ben just wasn't cut out for all that."

"Well, then he could have said something. And if he didn't it's his own fault! You know, I really just get so mad at him sometimes."

"Mad? How come?"

"Because he just left me to deal with all our family's shit all by myself. First he takes off and leaves home, and then he goes and checks out for good. And plus all those stupid drugs he took . . . doesn't it make you mad, too?"

"Sure. But I don't have a right to feel that way."

"Of course you do! I've read that anger is actually a part of the grieving process." Dorothea rolls her eyes and balls her fists. She's truly seething with rage now. "Sometimes I could really just . . . kill him!"

Clara's heart skips a beat. And the car starts to shudder as well—the engine stalled when she tried to put it in gear.

After two seconds of shocked silence they both look at each other. And suddenly they both have to laugh.

. . .

Somehow, once Dorothea made this plainly absurd comment, the tension was broken. They'd had a really pleasant afternoon together after that, thinks Clara as she lies in bed exhausted late that night. She's also glad that she found an appropriate moment to give Dorothea Ben's watch.

Today they had had more fun together than ever before. And yet they had also cried together. For example, as they stood on the St. Pauli piers staring out over the water at the opposite bank of the Elbe, Dorothea had gotten very quiet all of a sudden. When she blew her nose, Clara knew that she was crying, even without looking at her. She hadn't needed to. Clara understood. And little by little Dorothea began to talk about her first New Year's Eve without her parents. She was fifteen years old and incredibly proud because Ben had said he was going to take his little sister to Hamburg with him. The plan was to start out partying in St. Pauli with a few of his bandmates and then around midnight to make their way through the Freihafen and find a spot near the Stage Theater to get a better view of the big fireworks show on the harbor.

The two siblings had always gotten along well together, as far as Clara could tell. But they really didn't spend much time together.

Dorothea put it that way, too, more or less. She said she was incredibly sad because she'd always looked up to her brother so much. Now she was an only child, and she felt guilty because it seemed like she had made it through the whole business of their messed-up childhood better than her brother had. But then Ben had always seemed so strong. He'd been her rock, someone she could always depend on and who was always right there for her whenever things got rough.

She had said all of this in one long monologue, like a kind of eulogy, and Clara knew just what she was talking about. In that moment, she sensed quite clearly that she was the only person who Dorothea felt she could speak so openly with. And immediately she felt like an egotistical monster who until now had been so consumed with her own sadness and despair that she never truly realized that other people were also grieving.

And that's why Clara is so happy that she worked up the nerve to tell Dorothea about the texts. Ben's sister didn't think it was creepy or crazy at all, just kind of amusing. Clara felt encouraged to go on further and describe how the strange idea of sending Ben texts had come to her, and what a comforting ritual it had become for her by this point.

Clara also confessed that she'd gone back and buried Ben's cell phone in the grave with him. A warm, almost hopeful smile came to Dorothea's face. In that case, she said, she still had a chance to let her brother know how mad she was, and at the same time that she regretted not telling him nearly enough how much she loved him.

Clara pulls the duvet up higher now and can't help but smile at the thought that now Dorothea will be texting her brother every now and then and might also find a little comfort in it. And she's very glad that she hadn't been too afraid to share what she was thinking with Ben's sister. She'd opened up to her about things that otherwise she had only shared with Katja—and maybe her grandmother, if she felt brave enough. But with Dorothea it even felt right to tell her about the absurd stories that she had heard at some point about people whose loved ones had died. Ever since Ben's death these stories keep popping into her head more and more. Apparently there are people who experience a kind of surge of energy after they've lost the person they love.

Clara told Dorothea about the experience that her mother had apparently gone through with Clara's father, about ten days after his death. Karin took the ferry to Sweden as a way of trying to get some distance. While Clara went to live with Lisbeth and Willy for a time, her mother meant to use this trip through Scandinavia to try to leave all the pain behind her, at least for a little while. After all, she had cared for her husband for months and had had to witness his body's steady decline firsthand. Clara doesn't know, even today, if her parents' marriage was what you could call true love. But she can well imagine how difficult the loss must have been for her mother. And even if Karin is with someone else now, still Clara knows that what her parents had was very special. And even aside from that, a boring guy like Reinhard can't hold a candle to her father.

In any case, when Karin was standing on the deck of the ferry back then, it was already dark outside. A summer storm was raging over the ship; rain was pouring down everywhere and she couldn't see particularly well. She stood at the railing and watched the lightning flash on the horizon. But then suddenly a bolt of lightning struck right in front of her, and a short while later Karin was filled with a feeling of utter well-being, as if she could feel her husband very close to her again. So close, it was as if he had been transported into her body. The way her mother described it, for these few seconds or even minutes she felt happier than she'd ever felt. She believed that her husband or his energy or whatever was actually with her in this moment—in whichever way that might be. And this filled her with such a feeling of joy and peace that she lacked the words to really describe it. But still today when she talks about this feeling she experienced so vividly on the ferry, her eyes take on a lively gleam. And even though she knows it makes Clara uncomfortable every time she hears it, Karin never gets tired of emphasizing how important this experience was for her perspective on the world, for her journey toward faith, and for her hopes of making peace with death.

But when her mother went through the whole spiel again after Ben died, Clara just got furious. She couldn't believe that even in this moment of extreme crisis her mother was only interested in taking advantage of the situation to go on about her loony New Age bullshit.

And yet, in spite of herself, Clara has thought about it again and again recently. She can't get the idea out of her head that Ben might just be out there somewhere, just waiting for a good moment to reveal himself. That's partly why she was so frightened when the light just went out like that after the first text she sent to Ben. But she's afraid of telling her mother about it, because then the eerie side of the story would get even more real. Nevertheless, every day she hopes for another sign from Ben that he's doing all right, that he's looking out for her, and that he's going to let her know that someday everything is going to be okay again.

Even though Clara is feeling very close to Ben after spending the day with Dorothea and would like to text him to say something along those lines, she decides to keep her thoughts to herself. It does strike her as being kind of ridiculous, but tonight she'd like to let Dorothea go first and fill Ben in on the latest news.

sven

N ow I have to put up with being yelled at, too?" Sven says by way of greeting. Judging by the look on his face, it's almost as if he's proud of the fact.

"Good morning to you, too," Hilke tersely replies. "Did Breiding go off on you again?"

"No. A new text. Listen to this: *I'm so pissed at you I could kill you!* Crazy, right?"

"What did you do?" Hilke asks, grinning now.

"Your Honor, I am completely innocent," Sven declares, raising his right hand. "I was even particularly well-behaved this weekend!"

"Oh yeah? I don't believe you. But what else did Lilime write?"

"The death threat wasn't even from Lilime, it was from somebody named Theo."

"Let me see!"

Sven rolls his eyes, pulls up the message, and hands his phone to his colleague.

Hilke fumbles for her glasses and reads:

I'm so pissed at you I could kill you. 😡
But I love you so so much and I'll look
after Clara for you. Promise! Xoxo, Theo

"Clara, Theo, Lilime—very mysterious. Sounds almost like some-body cheated on somebody else and that person's friend is mad at the other person and that's why they're looking after Clara."

Sven acts like he's bored. "No idea. Couldn't care less, either. But if this keeps up I'm going to call the number and tell the guy to stop bothering me already!"

"And you're sure that Theo isn't Lilime, right?"

"What do I know? In any case this last text came from a differ-ent number."

"And who's No Name?" Hilke asks to Sven's surprise—apparently she's found her way to his Messages folder.

"All right, give it back!"

"Well, well, this is getting more and more interesting," says Hilke, ripping the lid off a yogurt cup like she's just settling in to watch a good show on television.

Sven puts his phone away and heads to the bathroom. *Why is this happening to me?* he asks himself, while in the stall next to his someone seems to be dealing with some digestive issues. He de-cides to do something productive once he gets off work tonight. *This week is going to be a damn blur,* he thinks. One meeting after the next. And so he now makes a firm plan to finally stop by his Tai Chi club again tonight.

The thought of it keeps him awake for the rest of the day. Sven is a bit anxious, though—he's afraid that after so much time away he won't see any familiar faces. Will his buddy David still be there? David was a university lecturer; Sven had gone out to eat with him a few times after class. But over the last few months Sven just hadn't made any effort to stay in touch.

And so he is all the more happy that evening when his old buddy walks right up to him and asks how he's doing, as if no time had passed.

That's exactly what he likes about David, the laid-back, uncomplicated manner he has about him. He's easygoing without having to put it on; that's just how he is. Plus he's got a great, bone-dry sense of humor. Without a second thought, Sven asks him if he wants to grab a bite to eat after class. They decide to treat themselves to a big platter of sushi and bring each other up to speed on what's been happening in their lives.

Sven feels uneasy at first. After all, it's not like he has any great achievements to report. He hasn't even started the triathlon training he'd made such a big deal about last time they spoke—four years since his last attempt, his goal is to try to reach the finish line in under four hours. If anything the opposite is true: Since Christmas Sven has gotten way out of shape and has actually put on weight. Not so much that his clothes no longer fit, but still enough that he no longer feels quite comfortable in his own skin.

So when the conversation starts he's all the more eager to listen. He's sincerely interested in what's new with David and encourages him to go first.

"Sven, I'm head over heels!" David blurts out as soon as they've ordered their maki.

Sven lets out a sigh and steels himself for what's coming. The truth is he hates hearing other people's meet-cute stories. But he actually is curious to hear how David—confident, only out for himself David—could bring himself to voluntarily give up his independence for a woman.

"She's just incredible. I never would have thought I'd make such a good catch!" David says proudly, as if he were speaking of a large pike that he'd braved the stormy seas to hook.

"Me neither," Sven admits, and David is a bit taken aback. "No, I mean, speaking of myself, I wouldn't ever think something like that would happen to me, either," he hastens to add.

David nods at him, full of understanding. Next ensues what for David is an unusually long monologue about women and men and about how he believes that every man is capable of falling in love, even the most dedicated bachelor. He lays out all his arguments with eyes shining and with such sincere enthusiasm that Sven can neither laugh nor come up with any kind of clever retort. Except to say that every infatuation eventually fades. But David won't have any of it. He ignores the comment in sublime fashion, as if it simply didn't merit a response. Instead he starts listing off details. His beloved's name is Stine, they've been together for two months now, and every day he finds her more desirable than ever.

"Desire . . . ," Sven suddenly hears himself saying—though this is something he'd rather not even think about. "Yes, I remember. That sure was something, wasn't it . . ." The whole "making love" thing, as Fiona always used to call it. That was wonderful, but he had shoved his awareness of it way back into the furthermost corner of his memory.

"So I guess your love life is super-exciting right now, huh?" David comments laconically.

Now Sven feels uncomfortable. He'd rather just ignore David's sarcastic remark. But David keeps looking at him, waiting for a response.

"Yeah, you know," Sven mutters, "it has been pretty dead lately."

David gets a sympathetic look on his face that hits Sven deep in the pit of his stomach. Quickly he adds: "But as of a few days ago I've got a secret admirer. Kind of a stalker, actually."

"You've got what?" David asks, amused.

"Well, I'm getting these text messages sent to my phone all the time from this person I don't know."

"And what does this mystery person want from you?"

"That's what I'd like to know," Sven replies and starts to relate the whole mysterious text business. Though of course he fudges some of the details a bit to suggest that Lilime is a woman and very much into him.

"But you don't know who this Lilime person is?" David asks, so interested now that Sven has to be careful in trying to navigate off the thin ice he's ventured out on.

"No, but there are a few girls who come to mind . . . ," Sven lies.

"Well, whoever it is you seem to be pretty taken with her," David teases. "Why don't you just call her and set up a blind date!" He's very excited about his idea and gives Sven a look, like he's daring him.

"Eh, we'll see. I'm not really into these silly little games," Sven says and tries to steer the conversation back to Stine.

With success: David talks so much about his scarcely imaginable stroke of luck that Sven is still thinking of it on his way home. Meeting a new flame over the internet would only make Sven mistrustful. After all, up to now he'd only used the web for fleeting hookups that ended either with the words "I'll call you!" or a bad taste in his mouth on the morning after upon waking up in a completely unfamiliar bed. He doubts that love can be found in any way other than the direct way, when you look very closely at another person and can feel the effect they have on you.

Should he really just call Lilime? he asks himself as he rides his bike home. Maybe there really is a woman hidden behind this mysterious number, a megababe like David's Stine. But even if that were the case, wooing her definitely wouldn't be easy. Sven tries to think how close the relationship might be between Lilime and the person who's actually supposed to be getting the texts. If the latter doesn't know how lucky he is, the whole thing might be more of a one-sided affair.

When Sven stops at the red light on Rödingsmarkt, he looks up at a lit-up billboard with a beer ad that shows a slick-looking guy having a good time. The man is relaxing on the couch, with his legs up on the coffee table and what is clearly a freshly poured glass of pilsner in his hand. Above him there's a tagline: "You only live once, boys!"

Now or never! The words flash into Sven's head. *I need a pay phone right away!* But as he's looking around for one he suddenly starts to feel pretty funny. After all, he is carrying a brand-new phone in his pocket, which can be used not only to take photos and listen to music but also—who'd've thunk it?—to call this damn number . . .

But there's no helping it. He wants to remain anonymous.

Suddenly Sven's heart starts pounding, but he tells himself that it's more from the quick burst of speed he just put on as he pedals toward the Reeperbahn than from the thing he's thinking of doing, which nothing in the world could justify being so excited about. He's about to run the red light at the next intersection, but then he stops and falls to thinking. On the one hand, he wonders if it's at all the right move to just call the number, and on the other, he's asking himself why he's even thinking about it in the first place. He decides that if he doesn't hit any more red lights on his way to St. Pauli, then he'll call the number. Otherwise he'll take the next red light to mean "Stop! Text back and delete the number!"

When Sven turns onto the Reeperbahn, he immediately catches

sight of two pay phones one next to the other on the right side of the street. He can't help but grin and wonders if his subconscious already knew that he would find what he was looking for here. Bit by bit, he's beginning to enjoy finding new little games for himself to play. He gets off his bicycle and starts digging in his pockets.

"If I've got the right change, I'll call right now!" he says to himself quietly and grins at the elderly lady at the phone next to his, who looks at him in bewilderment.

It must be an odd sight, he thinks—*a perfectly normal-looking man holding the receiver of a Telekom pay phone in one hand and a brand-new iPhone in the other.*

Hesitating, Sven takes another glance around him, as if he were about to call to blackmail someone and do the whole disguising-his-voice bit. But really all he's going to do is politely ask if—he thinks for a second—if David is there. Right, he'll ask if his friend David is there. And then Lilime will reply that there's no David here; this is Rolf, Egon, Hugo, or whoever.

Of course Sven is hoping that whoever picks up says their full name so he can do some actual research for once and maybe even gather some new material for his crime novel. But whatever the case he wants to finally start making a little progress with his "investigation."

Sven dials the number and waits anxiously for it to ring. And sure enough, after about five rings someone picks up: "You've reached the voice mailbox for: 0172 . . ."

"Shit!" Sven curses. It went to voice mail. He hadn't counted on that or at least not on an automated voice recording. He's angry. But not so much at the fact that he was only able to hear this robotic voice. No, he's more angry at himself and resolves to forget the whole thing as quickly as possible.

clara

After a long day, Clara snuggles up contentedly under Ben's duvet, whose cover she still hasn't washed, and types a text into her phone.

> Did you hear from Theo? You should be very proud of her. And maybe you're proud of me, too? Today I finished the moon painting, just for you. A thousand kisses!

She scrolls down for Ben's number and hits send. Even though spending the day with Dorothea yesterday was so nice, the unfinished canvas just wouldn't let her rest.

That same night, after they'd hung out, Clara had gotten right back to work on the newly begun painting that was meant to portray the far side of the moon.

She didn't think that she'd already be finished with it today. She could barely wait to get back from work and hurried to get home as fast as she could. She skipped dinner and even ignored her phone when it rang. But when she realized it could be Katja calling to spill the latest news about her lover boy, she ran out into the hallway. The voice mailbox was quicker, though. Whoever had called, they didn't leave a message, and Clara couldn't help thinking it could be another sign from Ben. After that she went back to working on her project with a smile on her face.

She sank deep into a wonderfully relaxed state. She was totally entranced. The brushstrokes came together almost of their own accord. Clara completely lost track of time and was shocked when she looked at the clock for the first time and saw that it was past midnight.

Even if it's only one painting for now, while she was working the idea occurred to her of making a whole series of moon paintings.

It's a nice thought, she mused—the thought of maybe one day getting a chance to exhibit her work somewhere. And who knows? Maybe there was even a way to earn a little money doing it.

Ben would definitely have been excited about this dream. As Clara stares into the darkness, she can see him quite clearly in her mind's eye—he sits on the kitchen table, casually props one leg on the table edge, and rolls himself a cigarette. "Hey, babe," he would say, "that's good. That's really good!" Then he would jump up, study the painting again very closely, act as if he were an art expert with shrewd business sense, and start talking, trying to convince Clara to commit to her dream, never stopping until Clara finally gave in and took the decisive step toward this new career.

Ben was always enthusiastic about everything. Whenever an idea came into his head, no matter how unrealistic it might be in practice, he would flesh it out in elaborate detail and take great joy in it. In this way a lot of conversations with him would end with him off dreaming. What started out as an ordinary, every-day topic could quickly turn into an effusive fantasy, whether it was his musical career and his band's meteoric rise to the top or a months-long trip around the world, which of course he didn't have a cent to spend on.

Tears come to Clara's eyes as she remembers this one-of-a-kind way he had about him. It's true that of late she hasn't been so quick to start crying when she thinks of Ben. But this in turn has only led to her being overtaken with ever more intense feelings of guilt, which she doesn't really know how to process. Even if Dr. Ferdinand did tell her at their very first session that feelings of guilt were totally normal for people who have lost loved ones, and were nevertheless completely unjustified, still her case is a bit different, she fears.

Maybe, at least unconsciously, she really did put too much pressure on Ben with all her hopes and ideas. Maybe he simply didn't want to disappoint her. Again and again she had needled him, before ultimately telling him more or less straight out that he finally had to start making progress with school if he ever wanted to get a decent job. First and foremost, of course, was the fact that she only wanted the best for him, which also included success in his professional life. But ultimately there was also a fair amount of egotism hidden behind this: her desire for a func-tional, storybook marriage, with a husband at her side whom she could rely on and who would have no problem supporting a family—even if she was frightfully aware of how conservative this was.

Maybe Ben only proposed to her so that she would finally give it a rest and stop trying to improve him, Clara thinks sometimes. And for a short time it worked really well. Clara felt like she was walking on air after Ben officially asked for her hand on Christmas

Eve. Right as her mother was bringing dessert to the table where her partner, Reinhard; Clara's grandparents; and Clara and Ben were gathered, Ben had stood up, tapped his spoon against his glass of red wine, and cleared his throat. Five pairs of eyes were looking at him, very eager to see what he had in store. Not even when he pulled out a small jewelry box did it occur to Clara what was coming. But when Ben finished his stiff speech and went down on one knee in front of Clara's chair, she finally realized what he was doing. With the most classic of words he asked, "Clara, will you marry me?"

Before she could even answer her mother had already started whooping and clapping with joy. Lisbeth and the men joined in and took turns hugging each of them tight once Clara finally managed to stammer out "Yes!"

But their happiness hadn't lasted long. Just a few weeks later the accident happened—and whether it was really an accident or not, Clara will probably never find out.

Clara stares off into space, twists the ring on her finger, and finally turns the light off. But it doesn't get truly dark. It must be a clear night tonight, with a full moon. In this silvery light, she can clearly make out Ben's smiling features in the photo she set out today. As if he were encouraging her, his great little artist, to make her moon painting project a reality, no matter what.

sven

The following Monday, Sven stares at his screensaver, lost in thought. He'd gotten to the office first thing that morning, before Hilke arrived, called customer service at the phone company, and said he was a business reporter and was conducting research for an article. He spoke confidently and energetically; the young man on the other end of the line provided answers in a credible and polite manner. It was just about impossible, technologically speaking, for text messages to be sent to two different recipients at the same time. Mix-ups between customers were extremely unlikely as well, the young man said, because a given cell phone number wasn't eligible to be reassigned until six months after the original contract had been terminated.

But it rankled Sven that he didn't manage to find out the name of the customer from whom all the texts were coming. He was told they couldn't make an exception, not even for a journalist. Discretion had to be maintained at all times when dealing with sensitive customer information.

"Why don't you just call the number and ask for the person's name?" asked the customer service rep, too smart for his own good.

All Sven could do in reply was make feeble excuses. He felt like a teenager who'd been caught peeping through a keyhole. He politely said thanks and quickly hung up.

"A cheerful good morning to you! What's the latest from Lilime?" asks Hilke as she hurries in the door, coffee in hand.

She seems to be just about bursting with curiosity. If she had her way, she would be informed immediately whenever a new text arrives. But Sven doesn't offer any information, he just grins at his coworker and replies: "Good morning to you, O favorite colleague of mine!"

Hilke stares at him, vexed, and impatiently drums her fingers on her desk.

"What's wrong?" Sven asks innocently.

"Nothing."

"Oh. Well, that's good then." Sven is still grinning.

After a few seconds of pretending to concentrate on the Post-it note that Breiding left on her computer, Hilke can't take it any longer: "Well, come on already, tell me! Don't make me force it out of you every time!"

"But there's nothing to force out, O colleague dear," Sven says smugly and enjoys his early advantage in this Monday morning contest.

"If you don't tell me right this instant what Lilime wrote over the weekend, I'll never have lunch with you again!" Hilke declares and leans back in her chair triumphantly as if she's just played an unbeatable trump card.

"Okay with me," Sven replies, and Hilke promptly throws a packet of tissues at him.

"Oooh, you little twerp! You can take your stupid text messages and stick them you-know-where!" Hilke yells.

Sven sits quietly and enjoys his triumph.

After a few minutes of cease-fire comes the next attack. "What

do I have to do to get you to give up your oh-so-secret information, dear Mr. Star Reporter?"

"Here," Sven says, calling a truce, and slides his iPhone to his
colleague across the desk. "If it'll make you stop bugging me!"

Satisfied, Hilke snatches Sven's phone and starts going through
Sven's messages with astonishing speed.

Sven tries not to let his nervousness show. It does make him
uneasy, though, to have a woman poking her nose into what is
currently his most intimate secret.

Hilke reads aloud:

> Darling, would you maybe like to
> tell me something? I've finished the
> second painting and am waiting for a
> sign from you. I love you, your L.

"I thought so! So No Name *is* Lilime after all. And Lilime
paints . . . how sweet! Oh, and this text here is also very revealing:
Did you hear from Theo? You should be very proud of her . . . So Theo's
not a man at all. Interesting!" Hilke is pleased with her research.
"Lilime is so romantic. These can only be coming from a woman!"

Sven's heart skips a beat. Or at least it feels that way for a brief
moment. He, too, has had a growing suspicion that behind Lilime there is actually a woman—a woman whose words move
him in a way he can't explain. But he can't possibly admit this to
Hilke. Romance or no romance.

"Do you know what? The whole thing is starting to get on my
nerves. I'm going to text back right now and tell this person that
to stop bothering me already!"

"No!" screams Hilke. "Then you'll never hear from her again."
Sven gives her a look, his head tilted to one side.

"Who knows?" Hilke says, pausing masterfully for effect. "Maybe she's the woman of your dreams!" And then she gets a big grin on her face.

Sven's heart skips another beat. First what David said leads him to waste his precious free time fantasizing about Lilime, and now Hilke is needling him about it at work.

"Right, and at the end of the story everybody loves everybody else and Hilke's faith in a good and just world has prevailed once again." Sven rolls his eyes.

"Yeah, so? What's so bad about that? And anyway, for somebody who's not at all interested in Lilime you sure get emotional about the whole thing," Hilke fires back.

Sven sees that he's been boxed into a corner and lets out a loud moan. But if he shows too strong a reaction now, then Hilke might think her analysis is right on target. He thinks for a second and then replies with almost a trace of pride: "All right, if you really want to know—I actually called the number last Monday to make it clear to this person that they were getting on my nerves."

"What? Really?" Hilke asks with a stunned look on her face and quickly adds, "And?"

"*And* nothing. Nobody picked up."

"Okay, but did it not go to voice mail?"

"Sure."

"Ugh, Svenny, you're driving me nuts! Come on, out with it!"

"Only if you stop calling me Svenny all the time!"

"Spill it already! Who is she, what's her name?"

"No idea."

"What do you mean, no idea?"

"The voice mailbox was automated."

"And?"

"What do you mean, *And?*"

"And? Did you leave a message?"

"No."

"Why not?"

"Because, that's why!"

"And how come you haven't tried again?"

Sven rolls his eyes again. "Why don't you do it!" he dares Hilke—and immediately feels like he could bite his tongue. Why would he say that?

"I'd be more than happy to," Hilke says cheerily. She seems barely able to fathom her good fortune.

"But hold on! Not with my phone."

"Oh, don't worry. I'll use mine."

She immediately reaches for her phone and dials the number. Sven, who can't bear to watch, shakes his head, grabs a folder full of papers, and says as he's leaving, "Good thing I have to go to the editorial meeting now!"

He's out the door and a few steps down the hallway before he realizes that he doesn't have a pen with him. He stops and considers whether he should go back to his desk to grab one, but hesitates—Hilke could interpret this as a mere pretense to disguise his curiosity and would use it against him. Of course he's interested in knowing if she manages to get through to Lilime and above all what this mysterious person might say. Slowly he walks back to his office, but he just stands outside the closed door. He looks around to make sure no one is watching him and tries hard to understand what Hilke is saying.

Unfortunately he can only make out a stray couple of words here and there: "Um . . . sorry . . . wrote it down wrong . . . oh, thanks . . . yes, you, too . . ."

Sven's heart is pounding. He feels completely ridiculous and would like to just walk right back into the office. But now he really needs to get to the conference room, he reminds himself, and hurries toward the stairs. He shakes his head again and again, and the cause isn't just his nosey coworker. No, it's himself above all, himself and his silly behavior.

. . .

When he finally gets back to his desk, Hilke is reveling in her victory. After letting him sweat a bit, making him ask her repeatedly over the course of a few minutes, she finally dishes out the hot scoop that Lilime is indeed very much a woman and on top of that has a warm and friendly voice.

"So anyway, we chatted a bit. I acted like I was trying to reach a certain Sven Breiding," she proudly declares.

Clearly she couldn't come up with anything more original at short notice than a combination of my name and our boss's, Sven thinks. And even though the conversation can't have lasted more than a few seconds, that doesn't stop Hilke from presenting him with a complete profile of Lilime's personality.

"She's definitely young. But not too young! I'd guess around thirty. She sounds well educated and north German. Or at least she doesn't have an accent and doesn't speak funny either . . . quite the opposite: Svenny, you should have heard her. A voice clear as a bell, with a note of melancholy in it, a very cultivated way of speaking . . . I almost want to say elegant!"

When Hilke goes on to ascribe sensuality and eroticism to the voice of the stranger on the telephone who reacted in such an exceedingly polite fashion to someone calling the wrong number, it finally gets to be too much for Sven. He heads out to lunch, shaking his head.

But as he's walking along the Elbe, he can't help but make his way straight to a pay phone. Even if he feels ridiculous, he just has to know if Hilke's assessment is even a little bit accurate.

But what is he supposed to say when Lilime picks up? Maybe he should try to get her caught up in a dull sales pitch. He could pretend to work at a call center. Maybe a kind of sweepstakes that he has to try to get her to take part in? She might even give him her personal information if his delivery sounds sufficiently believable. Then he would at least know who he was actually dealing with here.

Sven steps up to a pay phone, dials the number, and waits anxiously for it to start ringing. He clears his throat several times, but when he finally hears what is actually a very likable-sounding voice on the other end, he freezes up with fear.

"Yes?"

Contrary to the plan he had just come up with on the fly, Sven is suddenly incapable of uttering a single syllable.

After a brief pause the voice asks: "Hello?" And again after a few seconds: "Hello?" and "Who's there?"

But Sven still can't react. He's just about to hang up, like a pimply faced teenager, when Lilime asks, in a very quiet and hesitant voice: "Ben? Is that you maybe?"

Sven gets a terrible fright and finally slams the phone back down on the cradle as quickly as he can.

. . .

Sven spends the whole rest of the day trying to get his thoughts in order. Again and again he asks himself why this complete stranger has such a hold on him. And because he can find no answer that satisfies him, he resolves to approach this thing more thoroughly than he has before.

He begins by typing all of Lilime's texts into a Word document and marking all the facts that are revealed in them in bold. Once he's finished, he prints out the three letter-sized pages and puts them away for later. He'll need some peace and quiet to conduct his analysis.

He bikes home, opens a bottle of wheat beer, puts on the Pink Floyd album that is still sitting next to the record player, and flops down onto the couch with his feet up on the coffee table.

He sits there brooding. All right, so what do I actually know about this woman? I know she doesn't have many reasons to laugh right now, but that she does seem to have a romantic bent. Plus there's a grandpa whom she loves very much. She paints moon paintings and likes to dance.

Once more Sven reads the text that came in sometime last week, late at night:

> Right now I want to dance, dance, dance.
> Will you come dance with me, please, right
> this second? I want to see you again, hear
> you, smell you, taste you, and touch you.
> Just to touch you—that more than anything.

Sven asks himself if he's interested in this woman, even though—or precisely because—he knows so little about her. The thing about this whole business is that it invites him to imagine his way into the life of a stranger whose love seems strangely unfulfilled and yet so full of hope. Her deeply felt emotions leave an indelible impression on him. And at the same time, Sven can sense how the melancholy that is clearly palpable in every text somehow leaves him feeling upset. He wonders if Lilime might be some kind of sign from fate, telling him to straighten up his attitude a bit when it comes to women.

When he and Fiona first started dating, he had sent countless messages by text or email. As the months went by, though, this habit fell by the wayside, especially since there came a point where Sven no longer knew what he could say to her. Usually they discussed everything on the phone or when they were together in person, so if anything, having to stay in touch in the meantime seemed more annoying to him than meaningful.

Lilime's voice is still ringing in Sven's ears. Even if he only heard her say a few words today, he's certain that an "I love you" from her lips would sound totally different than it did coming from Fiona's. Different than how this worn-out line sounded in his memory.

Sven takes another sip and turns off his stereo; the record has long since ended. He feels uneasy and doesn't quite know why. Does he actually feel lonely? Before today he's never asked himself that question.

Looking through his notes again Sven realizes that the tone of Lilime's texts in the past few days is noticeably brighter, less heavy with sadness and longing. For what it's worth, he also knows by this point that her job might have something to do with advertising and that she seems to be successful in her work but not especially happy. Besides that, he knows that her world contains a Clara, a Katja, a Karin, a Knut, a Theo, and a Carsten, as well as a Grandpa and Grandma. A lot of it revolves around profound questions and speculation. Lilime seems to miss a man whom she loves but can't have for some reason. Maybe, Sven conjectures, he works on an oil platform in the North Sea, or he's on a research expedition to the North Pole—after all, Lilime has referred to someplace "up there" in a lot of the texts.

But maybe the person the texts are meant for simply doesn't exist. Maybe he's dead, lying in a coma, or is a kind of made-up figure. Like a dream man that Lilime has created in order to escape her dreary everyday life, which seems to consist exclusively of obnoxious clients, meaningless ad campaigns, socially inept coworkers, and too many long hours. And so she just typed in the phone number at random. Maybe she hopes it will lead to some exciting adventure, like a small child, full of eagerness and expectation, who puts a message in a bottle and tosses it into the ocean.

But then again, Lilime doesn't really seem naive or immature. The language she uses makes her seem very grown up, even if it is a bit pretentious at times. At any rate, she is clearly a person with many different facets, which sometimes seem to contradict one another. So on the one hand, Lilime seems very driven, ambitious, and grounded. And on the other, Sven believes he recognizes in her a woman who is full of melancholy, romance, and a very special tenderness.

What does she look like? he wonders and takes a long sip of beer. He'd be into a Lilime with large breasts and long legs and long, wavy, chestnut-brown hair. A bit like Fiona. But he would guess that Lilime is more on the petite side and has delicate facial features, the kind that seem to express many things at once. She seems to be rather unsure of herself and definitely does not have her life under control. That would seem to suggest more of a short, nondescript person, a bit less than attractive, the kind of person he would pass by on the street without noticing. But if he happened to get into a conversation with her, she would definitely be able to make up for her unremarkable looks with her sensitive nature and her intellect.

Sven can't help grinning at the thought that he himself is well on his way to creating a kind of dream woman, and that in his imagination he allows her to get much closer to him than he would ever permit any of the real women he's shared his bed with lately. When it comes down to it, Lilime doesn't bother him and she doesn't make any demands. Her texts are an interesting source of entertainment. But still, Lilime's voice is real. And that means she really exists.

Sven just has to find her.

clara

Feeling morose despite the July sun, Clara stands at the kitchen window and keeps a lookout for Katja's brand-new Fiat 500.

"We'll take a test-drive this weekend. To Hamburg. But only if you get nice and dolled up like you used to!" her friend had warned.

The thing is, this Saturday had actually started out quite promising. In the morning Clara had gone on a tear through the shops in Lüneburg's beautiful Old City for the first time in months and had had a real blast spending money. She'd gotten two pairs of jeans, a flashy top, and a marked-down but still murderously expensive pair of summer shoes that look very elegant and are a fairly big departure from her normal style.

At first Clara had been looking forward to being in a suitable atmosphere to show off her new clothes. But now she would much rather stay home, drink a glass of wine, listen to some nice music, and work on her paintings some more.

But if she cancels on Katja one more time she's going to have to start looking for a new best friend soon. Even though Katja, by her standards anyway, had had a very rough time dealing with the aftermath of the Robert affair, Clara hadn't been much help to her. Every time her friend wanted to try to get her mind off Robert by going out to a cocktail bar or to see a movie, the effort foundered in the face of Clara's unwillingness to be among people. Grief makes you egotistical. But if nothing else, Clara never stops trying to cheer Katja up. After all, Robert actually did leave his wife, or at least he claims he did. But as yet Katja hasn't deigned to see him more than twice. Instead she decided to buy herself a new car.

"It's such an exhilarating feeling!" Katja says excitedly when Clara finally climbs into the robin's-egg-blue Fiat. "You should try treating yourself to something really, really swanky."

"Already did," Clara responds proudly and lifts her right foot so that Katja can admire her new shoes.

"Wow! New?" Katja asks.

"Brand new. It's been eons, but I finally went out and did some real intense shopping."

"That is a damn good sign, babe. And it's also high time we had some fun together again. Just you wait, this is going to be a sensational evening!"

"So tell me, what is it you actually plan to do with me?"

"Nothing in particular," Katja singsongs in such an exaggeratedly casual way that Clara immediately gets suspicious.

"Come on, tell me! You're cooking something up, I know it. We're going to a strip club in St. Pauli, is that it?" Clara asks, trying to head off right here at the outset her very worst fear of what a Saturday night might have in store.

But Katja only grins, which makes Clara even more suspicious. "Why do I get the feeling that I'm going to have to do something tonight that I've never done before?"

"Well, that's easy, because you're about to take this sweet car for a spin as soon as we fill up the tank."

Clara grins back and is already looking forward to the test-drive. But there's something else in the works here. Something that makes her feel very uncomfortable.

...

Even though Clara hates to let a warm summer Sunday just slip by like this, it's already mid-afternoon and she still hasn't managed to do anything productive. She sits at the table on her little balcony as if in a trance, flipping through a magazine whose contents are of absolutely no interest to her.

Her thoughts keep straying back to last night. How could Katja do that to her? Of course she'd totally meant well. But it just wasn't the right time. For Clara it felt like it came about three years too early.

It wasn't an exaggeration to say that until this weekend she had never, not once, seriously entertained the thought of going on a date with another man, to say nothing of getting involved with one. Just the thought of kissing strange lips, lying in a new man's arms, or smelling a completely unfamiliar body makes Clara shudder. Even if she has enough experience to know that every heartache eases sooner or later, no matter how great, she can't imagine ever being able to love someone other than Ben for the rest of her life.

And then Katja goes and introduces her to not just one guy but eight at the same time!

When she and Katja walked into the bar on the Binnenalster

and her friend led her to a separate room in which five men and three women were already seated, Clara didn't yet suspect what the actual purpose of this outing was. Only when the moderator handed her a form and she saw the words "Speed Dating 8×8×8" printed at the top did things start to click for her. Never would she have thought that Katja, without her knowledge, would force her to take part in such an event. Before now Clara had taken for granted that she would never have to put herself up on the market like this.

Katja of course thought it was a super idea and just kept winking at her with a big grin on her face every time the men switched to the next table after eight minutes of the most superficial chitchat.

Granted, Clara had actually enjoyed—just the tiniest little bit—receiving nice compliments from this or that guy. But afterward she was plagued with guilt. And when she got back home she couldn't even bring herself to text Ben. She simply didn't know how to confess to him that she had gone out looking for a man. And the thing was, none of the candidates had turned out to be nearly as attractive or charming as Ben, not even close. With the exception of the genial moderator Andreas, who always kept up a positive mood and wore a very conspicuous wedding ring, all the guys tended to be more on the pathetic side, longtime loners who hid their desperation behind hectic questions and what were supposed to be confident gestures.

Sure, she and Katja did have a lot of fun. But really the fun only came after this lame event was over, when they got to run through and comment on the performance of each of the male—and female—candidates. Dieter, for example: forty-six, balding, sweaty palms. He'd actually asked Katja and Clara the exact same questions, as if he'd written them all down beforehand and learned them by heart. And Florian, who was actually a strapping young guy in his midtwenties, but who unfortunately tended to spit when he talked. Volker on the other hand barely managed to say a word and maintained eye contact exclusively with her chest.

From the get-go, Clara refused to even consider going on a date and didn't want to give her email address out either. She just didn't see any point in going out with a man when she already knew that she would spend the whole evening trying desperately and with great effort not to bring up the things that were most on her mind at the moment. This being the case, she didn't want to fake any interest and therefore told all the candidates that the only reason she was there in the first place was that she was doing her friend sitting at the next table a favor—and a questionable favor at that.

Clara was a bit afraid that Katja was secretly disappointed by the evening's meager yield. But Katja wouldn't be Katja if she didn't turn a setback into a victory. She immediately set out to get the scoop on this Andreas guy. Clara did have to admit that he was incredibly attractive and totally confident, too. When he was explaining the rules, he demonstrated a subtle sense of humor that definitely lent the event a touch of class. Katja finally ended up asking him straight out if she could also put him on her list of guys who should get her number. But he just smiled and said ambiguously: "Oh, but you've got my number already . . ." Katja took this to be a clear invitation to take action.

Clara is positive that over the next couple of weeks her friend is going to make a gigantic fuss over this guy. After all, they were in their prime, Katja said, which meant they should go looking for the best, no matter how much baggage, past or present, might happen to come with it.

Now Clara can't help but smile at the thought of how much energy her total whack job of a friend has put into trying to get some life back into her in any way possible. Clara loves her for it. And for putting up with her passivity and fearfulness. And for always coming up with hundreds of ways to have fun and get their minds off things.

But Katja is going to have to accept that she and Clara will never again have the kind of silly conversations about men and relationships that they used to have. How can anything ever be light and cheerful again when there's this ever-present doubt like a little gnome sitting in Clara's ear, whispering "Nothing is as it seems," "You can never trust this peaceful feeling," and even "Maybe you don't deserve happiness"?

Clara just doesn't like herself anymore. Sometimes she wishes someone would just get right up in her face and yell at her, tell her that she should quit wallowing in self-pity already and stop idealizing Ben. But instead of this, not only her grandparents but also her friends, her coworkers, and of course her mother as well are constantly trying to cheer her up. Really though there's only one thing Clara wants: to be her old self again. She wants to be rid of this stigma that it seems like everyone can spot from ten yards off and that makes her feel like she has something sinister or malign clinging to her.

Clara keeps flipping listlessly through the pages of the magazine until suddenly an ad catches her eye that she remembers seeing last night on a billboard on the way into Hamburg. It's not particularly well put together in terms of the visuals, but the slogan does bring a little grin to Clara's face. A hip-looking guy sits relaxing on the couch and enjoying a beer. Above him is the slogan: "You only live once, boys!"

Just as she did yesterday, Clara immediately thinks about how Ben, too, had had only one life, a life that might have been far too short but that he tried harder to enjoy than anyone else she knew.

But what about her? Could it be that when his life ended, hers did, too, just like that? Clara sits up. That can't be true; she can't let it be true. No matter what the actual cause of Ben's death was, he wouldn't have wanted Clara to remain unhappy on his account. And even if for some reason that is what he wanted, she still has every right to enjoy life as best she could.

Little by little a kind of furious anger rises within her. Anger at life, at her fate, and sometimes at Ben, too. It would be nice if one day she were to meet someone who could deal with her and what she's been through without being embarrassed or awkward about it, someone who sees only her and isn't scared off by her history.

Clara goes to the kitchen to get something to drink. Her eye catches the card from the pizza delivery place that's pinned to the fridge with a magnet. She feels a lump forming in her throat: Almost every Sunday night, Ben had ordered dinner there for the two of them. And suddenly Clara has a huge craving for a real greasy, salty pepperoni pizza with a thick layer of cheese.

She reaches for the phone, places her order, and gives a start when the person on the other end asks if the address is still the same and if the order is for "Runge, Benjamin Runge."

"No!" Clara responds, instantly aware of how horribly impolite she sounds. "You can cross Runge out. But the address is correct; the delivery is for Sommerfeld."

When she hangs up, Clara considers for a second whether she

should give in to the impulse that the knot in her throat triggers in her. But she doesn't want to start crying yet again. She doesn't want to have to put this weekend down as a defeat; rather she wants to summon all her strength and call it progress. And so she heads back out on her now very shady balcony and tries to look forward to her first pizza in almost half a year.

sven

As far as Sven is concerned, his "investigations" in the Lilime case are far from being wrapped up, but thanks to a rough week at work they've definitely been forced to take a backseat for the past few days. In that time, Sven has started to wonder if losing himself in this silly fantasy world with Lilime isn't serving as a convenient excuse for not finding some other way to take control of his life. Somehow he's gotten stuck in his same old rut, nothing but deadlines and meetings, and he feels more than ready for a vacation. His life of late feels like a corset.

And the thing is, he actually loves his job! He likes to write, and he likes the hectic pace, too, when it comes down to it. He likes his apartment as well; he feels comfortable in it. And even his last visit with his father was surprisingly pleasant and uncomplicated, and left Sven with the feeling that they were slowly starting to grow closer.

Sven goes to the refrigerator to look for something tasty for dinner, trying to head off the gloomy mood he feels coming on. But finding neither frozen pizza nor anything else edible—or at least that he feels like eating—he decides to head back out onto the street.

He grabs a large bag to throw away everything that he knows he's never going to eat. This tube of tomato paste doesn't just have a disgusting crust around the cap, it also expired more than a year ago, Sven registers to his astonishment. And he's better off not looking all too closely at these two jars of marmalade. As far as Sven can remember, they were presents from Fiona's mother. But he doesn't even like marmalade—and he definitely doesn't like this disgusting salad dressing that Fiona loved so much. The bottle is now undoubtedly host to an amazingly diverse array of mold cultures.

It's high time for my ex-girlfriend to clear out of my apartment for good, he thinks. *And today's a good day for it!*

Spirits high, he takes the already half-full bag and casts his gaze around the loft, looking to eliminate any and all mementos from his days with Fiona. There aren't many left to begin with: a goofy postcard on the dresser, a fruit bowl that he never liked in the first place, a jar of bath salts that is just collecting dust, a few clothes, a few pairs of shoes, a corny gingerbread heart from the Hamburg fair, and finally a few unframed photos in a drawer. The photos he'd like to keep. But everything else he stuffs into the bag without a single pang of regret.

Next he grabs his wallet, his keys, and his phone, and he's out the door. The night will take him first to the trash bins, then to the gourmet section of the supermarket, and finally to the video store.

clara

The path from the cemetery entrance to Ben's grave seems interminably long. Clara feels very ill at ease and can't quite figure out if it's because she just fundamentally hates being so near to Ben's dead body or if it's that her mother insisted on coming with her today.

"How often are you coming here these days?" Karin now asks. Her tone of voice is gentle and subdued, but even still, Clara immediately feels like she's been put on the defensive. She feels guilty because in the past few weeks she has very rarely found the courage to come here.

"It's hard for me. This place gives me the creeps."

"But that's perfectly all right." Her mother hesitates, but then links arms with Clara and adds carefully: "This fear of yours probably means that you've still got a lot left to work through."

"Yeah, yeah. I know," Clara replies. She has to stop herself from immediately snapping at her mother.

"But you know I'm always here for you, honey." Unasked, her mother continues speaking: "There are so many things we can do to make your pain a little easier to bear. But the most important thing is, you have to let go!"

"I'm perfectly aware of that. But it doesn't help that you keep harping on it all the time." Clara tries to stay calm, but inside she's already lost it.

"I just want to help you. What kind of mother would I be if I didn't share with you my own valuable experiences of dealing with grief?"

Clara shakes her head and decides to just not say anything. What she really wants right now is to be alone. Alone and some-place far away from here.

Again and again, the thought of just taking off pops into her head. Drop everything, run away, and start fresh somewhere else. No doubt her mother would only interpret these thoughts as being indicative of a desire on Clara's part to flee from her own painful reality. She would give her a long sentimental speech trying to convince her to undergo a holistic therapy regimen and finally align herself with the energy of the universe. She would drag out all her slick self-help books again and list off the addresses of countless experts whom Clara could turn to in confidence for help finding her way back to herself and regaining her inner strength.

During such conversations, Clara would like nothing more than to scream and shout and tell her mother right to her face that maybe she never had any inner strength to begin with and that the reasons for this were no doubt to be found in her childhood. After her father died, Clara felt completely alone in her grief. She almost never saw her mother crying for him. And now, when she just wants to be left alone, Karin thinks she has the right to probe deep down inside her, and all she ends up doing is rubbing more salt in her wounds.

"Oh, these are beautiful!" her mother exclaims when she sees the white bouquet of gerbera and roses that has been left at the base of the headstone. "You didn't bring these here, did you?"

Again Clara gives a shudder on the inside. At first she wants to respond with a defiant no, but then she says only: "I'm sure they're from Dorothea or her mother."

Suddenly Karin pulls a glass figurine from her handbag. Only when Clara looks closer does she see that it's an angel.

"What are you going to do with that?" she asks in surprise.

"Here, take a closer look!" Karin points at the face of the figurine. "The angel is singing and looks so cheerful. I found it in that cute shop on Schröderstrasse and immediately thought of Ben."

Clara gives her mother a skeptical look. But Karin just smiles.

"If it's all right with you, I thought I'd leave it here," she says finally, then she places the figurine at the base of the headstone next to the flowers and steps back again.

"You never brought anything to leave at Dad's grave . . . ," Clara suddenly hears herself saying.

Her mother looks taken aback. "But for a long time I had that place on the dresser in the bedroom where I would put everything."

Clara feels a twinge of pain. Except for the photo on her nightstand, she doesn't really have any place dedicated to Ben or her memories of him.

Carefully Clara's mother puts her arm around her shoulder. And after they've stood there for a long time staring in silence at the inscription on the gravestone, Karin says quietly: "You know, I loved him, too. Ben really came to be quite dear to me. You're not alone in your grief."

Clara doesn't know what to say. She feels a knot in her throat and swallows hard, but she doesn't let anything show.

. . .

Only looking back at it late that night, after she and her mother had had a very relaxed dinner together—just some spaghetti with pesto and parmesan—and talked a bit about how bad the mood at the agency had been of late, does the day Clara spent with her mother seem to have turned out halfway bearable.

Clara had imagined the trip to the graveyard going much worse. But today she had even admitted to her mother that she was very glad, thinking back on it now, that she had taken the opportunity to say goodbye to Ben in the chapel on the day of the funeral. It had been Karin who had gently encouraged her to do so. She said it would be very comforting for her to be able to see with her own eyes that the soul had left the body. Having to get through the funeral and to see the casket being lowered into the ground was bound to be less painful for Clara if she knew that it was "only" the body that was being buried.

And in fact Clara had scarcely been able to recognize the Ben she knew so well. Despite the head injury that he'd suffered, succumbing immediately upon impact, he looked unhurt and very peaceful, almost relieved even. But on the other hand Clara wasn't able to see anything in his face that could have revealed something of his true personality. It was only his hands, lying folded across his chest, that left Clara with a pain that is still with her, that she can still feel deep down.

Even though she misses the smell of him, his voice, his warmth— even though she misses everything so much, it is his hands that are most symbolic to Clara of the unspeakable loss she suffered with his death. They're simply no longer there for her to touch, they're no longer tender, they no longer provide comfort—they no longer move, even though, lifeless as they were that day, they looked nearly as gentle and familiar to her as before.

So many times Clara had watched Ben play guitar, his beautiful, strong, and yet somehow delicate fingers plucking the strings. There were times when he would sit for hours on the floor in the living room and just play. Favorite songs that he'd play from memory, more difficult pieces that he'd pick out with the help of sheet music, and above all little disjointed parts that he would play over and over again, working through countless variations, till finally he had shaped them into a new, wonderful song that was wholly his own.

Clara can't help but smile when she thinks of it now. She makes a plan for this coming weekend to listen to all of his CDs, organize them, and maybe give a few of them to Knut and the guys.

She feels like it's getting to be about time for her to tell Ben a little about the difficult but also kind of nice day she had. Clara turns on her phone—she'd kept it off all day today—and with a sad smile, starts typing.

sven

There are few things that Sven hates more than stuffy hotel rooms. Which makes it all the more annoying that his old college buddy Philipp from Berlin picked this of all weeks to be out of town. If he were here, Sven would no doubt be out hitting the bars in Friedrichshain with him, despite having an early meeting tomorrow, and not here in this faux-fancy dump near Kurfürstendamm. Really Sven should be preparing for the two interviews he has tomorrow, which, between the preparation, the interviews themselves, and all the work to be done on them afterward, are bound to spoil his whole week. But on the train ride here it had been impossible for him to concentrate on anything. And now, too, his thoughts keep drifting off.

He's rather on edge, and he couldn't even say what the reason is, whether it's this small room and the far too greasy dinner he just had or the fact that it's raining and he can't motivate himself to go out and get a bit of Berlin air in his lungs.

He hasn't been in the best of moods lately anyway. It's clear to him that the lack of texts from Lilime is making him nervous somehow. It's been days. During the train ride he was this close to sending her a text, just a polite note to ask why he hadn't heard from her in so long. But he couldn't think of anything that wouldn't have immediately scared Lilime off.

He wonders what could have happened. Maybe she finally discovered her mistake and now knows that the texts aren't going to the person they're meant for. Maybe her boyfriend is back from his trip and there's no reason to keep fawning over him. Or maybe something happened to her. Maybe she's fallen out of love. Maybe . . .

Maybe he couldn't care less about any of it!

Sven sits down on the hard bed, reaches for the remote to turn the TV on, and at the same time gets out his notes and the research he's put together. He's a bit angry at himself for not bringing a good book with him. But he knew that if he had he wouldn't concentrate on his actual job.

After ten minutes of trying in vain to give the notes his full attention, he puts the TV on mute. Time keeps slipping past, and Sven's uneasiness grows.

He reaches for his iPhone and scrolls through his contacts. Maybe he should call David again to ask how things are going with his new flame. But the truth is he's not at all interested. And that's exactly what he most dislikes about himself these days: Whether it's his friend David or Hilke at work, he has a hard time being happy for other people. He used to be far more easygoing; envy wasn't a big thing with him. If something really great happened to somebody else, he was of course a bit envious, but he never felt any resentment. The way he's been lately, though, if he were to ask David about his new girlfriend, he'd secretly be hoping that she was out of the picture.

Thoughts like that are just sick, he rebukes himself. *And this is even sicker*, he thinks, as he reads Lilime's number off his phone in order to dial it on the keypad of the phone in his room. He does it very slowly. Like a little boy playing with fire. First he hesitates, then he takes the bold first step, only to immediately shrink back again, second-guessing—until finally courage and curiosity win out.

Sven doesn't understand why he feels such an urge to make contact with an imaginary woman.

But he can't help it. It's time to finally take action instead of constantly weighing all the arguments—rational, minutely detailed—that speak for or against it.

It's ringing.

Sven can feel his heart pounding. He sits up ramrod straight on the bed, clears his throat, and feels completely ridiculous.

"You've reached the voice mailbox for: 0172 . . ."

Disappointment and relief flood through him. Voicemail again, popping up like an insurmountable barrier between reality and the world of illusion. Like a sign telling him he'd better forget Lilime.

Sven sits there thinking.

Suddenly he jumps up, pulls on a hoodie, and heads outside—he will take that walk after all.

• • •

"Great. So our sushi place in half an hour?" Sven asks his friend David on the phone the next afternoon.

"Sounds good. Looking forward to it!" David replies.

Even though Sven is totally wiped after the train ride back to Hamburg, he just has to talk to a halfway rational person, someone he can hash things out with. Today was a sheer nightmare.

Two long interviews with pompous CEOs who talked his ear off. One of the interviews took place over lunch, just to make things more stressful. Meanwhile his thoughts were only ever on Lilime and her text and this very strange moment that occurred after his walk in Berlin last night.

Almost as if he'd been expecting it, the first thing he did when he got back to his hotel room was glance over at his phone. He couldn't find the nerve to really look at first—it just seemed humiliating to him to wait around for a text that wouldn't come. And how could he actually feel hurt or disappointed when the texts were clearly meant for someone else? But when he was holding the phone in his hands, Sven suddenly had a feeling of certainty. Almost like when you feel relaxed going into a job interview or an exam, sensing that things are guaranteed to go well.

When he saw that it actually was a text from No Name, he felt a mild shock at first—he was simply taken aback by this giant coincidence. The apt timing made it seem almost magical to him. After all, just moments before, as Sven was walking down Ku'damm, he had sworn to himself that he would finally ditch this fantasy named Lilime unless he heard from her this same night. And then the next thing he knew, all he felt was joy and excitement—the long radio silence had been broken.

But when Sven read what was written, he was confused at first. He had to read through a second time before he finally realized what had just been revealed to him. Lilime wrote:

> I went to see you, at your grave. And yet you were so far away. Can things ever be good again? Without you, your hands, your music? With love, L.

Now Sven, still wearing his suit, sits at home on his roof terrace. He stares up at the deep blue sky, at the white shapes of the clouds floating past. He loosens his annoying tie and takes out the list of all the texts from the past few months. Even if he's speculated dozens of times about whether the man Lilime loved might no longer be alive, it seems eerie somehow to see his hypothesis confirmed, as if he himself were solely responsible; as if his fantasies had made it happen.

Maybe this is my conscience finally making itself heard, he thinks. Because during the train ride back from Berlin he definitely started to experience something like joy. Joy at finding out that Lilime wasn't spoken for.

But her heart is. Her heart is clearly spoken for! And this again becomes very apparent to Sven as he reads through all the texts one after another.

He stands up and leans against the railing. From here he has the best view over the rooftops of the city.

It's unusually warm this evening, and Sven hopes he'll still be able to snag a table outside for him and David. Otherwise he'll suggest they give the sushi bar a pass and head to a beer garden instead. The main thing is that they stay out in the fresh air and don't waste this balmy night being cooped up inside some stuffy restaurant.

Sven is thinking about what to wear tonight when suddenly he realizes that he's breathing heavily; it's like he can't get any air in his lungs. He's noticed himself having these bouts of shortness of breath for some time now. At first he thought it happened today only because he'd climbed the stairs a bit faster than usual—he was in a hurry to get to the list of Lilime's texts. But his breathing should have gone back to normal by now. And still he just feels keyed up inside, nervous almost.

There's nothing for it. Even if it means looking ridiculous, Sven thinks, he has to talk to David about this whole thing. He's spent so much time thinking about it, going back and forth and back and forth, that he simply doesn't know what's what anymore. He just hates being in situations where he's not in control. And this situation is too much for him.

What should he do? Should he try to ignore Lilime? Should he ask her—politely, but firmly—to stop sending him texts? Should he get a new number so he can just contact her out of the blue? But what then? Should he just call her up and ask her out for coffee so they can have a completely absurd and unwanted chat about how she lost a person she loved? Should he track her down in secret and make a fool of himself that way?

For a brief moment Sven hesitates. Maybe he'd better tell David he can't make it tonight. But if he doesn't leave the house now, he's just going to wallow in the same wearying thoughts that won't get him anywhere.

Newly determined, Sven marches into the bedroom. He gets undressed, hops into the shower, and tries to figure out the best way to update his friend in on the situation—hopefully he won't look like too much of a dope.

clara

üneburg is actually wonderful, thinks Clara as she rides her bike through the Kurpark on Friday evening. It might take a lot longer than her usual route home from the agency, but on a warm summer evening like this one, it's totally worth it.

Up until recently it was very hard for her to leave work in the evenings and head back home, knowing that no one was waiting for her there. But at this point the mood among her coworkers is so strained and hostile that she doesn't like being there at all anymore. A few important commissions have fallen through recently, and a lot of her coworkers are starting to get seriously worried. Maybe she should start sending out a few applications herself? She has been seeing occasional job postings online and in the newspaper, which suggests that the market for graphic designers maybe isn't as overrun as she thought. Who knows what might be out there? On the other hand, though, Clara doesn't have much experience outside the agency, so she can't boast of having worked on big campaigns for prominent clients.

Besides, she would much rather earn her money painting. That's not especially realistic, of course—there's no doubt about that. But she could try to make a little money on the side. She could hold courses to teach painting to people who are interested in doing it as a hobby. By this point Clara has developed her own technique using a special kind of sheet metal and other materials from the hardware store. The combination of oil paint and metal elements lends her paintings a very special quality. Katja and her mother have said so, too. Not that their opinion is particularly objective.

And now it's finally the weekend! And Clara is looking forward to having two days off. It'll be the right mixture of excitement and relaxation; other than going to see her grandparents she doesn't have anything planned except to paint as much as she feels like—hopefully this way she can stop brooding, for a while at least.

It's still very hard for her to switch off. Normally there's something in her head that just puts her on alert about ten times every hour. Out of the blue, her brain will start flashing a message in big bright letters in front of her mind's eye: "Ben is dead!"—as if the regular reminder were at all necessary.

But even if she really wanted to, it would be simply impossible for Clara to consciously put what happened and what she's lost out of her mind for even a short period of time. This is her "life" now, and in all likelihood it will be this way till the end. Like having tinnitus and hearing a shrill ringing in your ears that is only drowned out on rare occasions. Supposedly it only stops completely when you're sleeping, if that.

There just has to be another way in this life, Clara thinks. *Even if Ben couldn't find it, I have to do everything I can to make sure his death doesn't end up being even more senseless.*

On bad days when she was a child, she would always create something pretty. She would crawl into the little fort she'd built for herself under the roof beams in the corner of her room and would sit there for a long time, dreaming: of a bigger room, a pet, a racing bike, or a princess dress, anything, until her tears dried up and she felt like taking her crayons and putting all the dream images in her head onto the page.

That's exactly what she'll do this weekend. She'll complete her seventh painting while listening to all of Ben's music, and in the time she has to spare she'll treat herself to lots of sunshine and fresh air and do a little research into ways she might be able to approach her painting a little more professionally.

sven

How romantic!" cries Hilke as she looks dreamily out the window. Then she lets out a rather loud sigh.

"What's so romantic about a young woman losing the love of her life?" Sven asks angrily. Dinner with David was pleasant enough, but didn't produce much in the way of results on the Lilime front, and so, on this Friday morning, Sven has swallowed all his pride and asked Hilke to give him her opinion.

"Ugh, it's so typical that I have to explain this to you yet again. You simply don't have a clue. This is pure romance. This is life!"

"I'm not so sure how death and life are supposed to link up here," Sven responds in a tone of voice that he hopes will put an end to this tiresome discussion of the latest news from Lilime's parallel world.

But apparently it only makes Hilke feel even more inspired to dispense her clever bits of wisdom about life and love. She leans back and breathes in deep: "Svenny!"

"What, Hilkie!?"

"Stupid man! Okay, so Lilime is basically, like, ultra-romantic. Just think about it for a second! How much pain and longing must she feel if the only remedy she can think of is to send messages to her lost love somewhere out there in the beyond?"

"It's bonkers and corny, if you ask me."

"Well, I didn't ask you! Because you have no sense of what truly matters in life. And you don't even deserve Lilime!"

Sven almost drops his coffee mug. He stares at Hilke in bewilderment. "I don't *what*? Now you've gone completely nuts!"

"Don't you see that fate has served you up a dream woman on a silver platter?!"

"A dream woman whose heart will be pining for someone else for the rest of her life."

"How do you know that? My cousin married again after her first husband died in an accident, and she's happy. But people like her take much more care with their newfound happiness, because they know how precious it is."

"Oh ho ho. Such big talk for so early in the morning . . ."

"Oh ho ho. Such small-mindedness for such a big manly brain . . ."

Sven wants to respond, but he can't come up with anything. And so he tries to focus on his interviews again, which still need work. And Hilke, too, turns back to her screen with a stern look on her face and starts wildly pounding away at her keyboard.

Even though he has already transcribed the most important parts from the MP3 files and inserted the quotes into his article, Sven stuffs his earbuds into his ears again to send a clear message to his colleague that she should spare him her blabbering already.

But Hilke won't drop it, and now she pipes up again via email. Sven tries to suppress a groan of annoyance when he sees the little Outlook window pop up on his screen.

From: Hilke Schneider

Subject: Deal

Dear Svenny! ☺ Ok. I've gotten the message and I propose a deal. I'll never stick my nose in your little affairs of the heart again, but only if you demonstrate that you actually have a heart!

Yours truly, H.

Sven can't help himself. He immediately clicks Reply:

From: Sven Lehmann

My dear Hilkie! Perfect—keep out of it!

Regards, S.

It takes Hilke less than a minute to respond. She, too, makes every effort to keep her eyes glued to her monitor and her face blank:

From: Hilke Schneider

Ok, but first you have to promise that you'll try to track her down.

From: Sven Lehmann

This is workplace harassment!

From: Hilke Schneider

So is having to look at your depressed face all the time!

From: Sven Lehmann

Leaving aside the fact that I don't actually want to meet her in the first place, I wouldn't even know how to track her down.

From: Hilke Schneider

You're a reporter at a renowned news magazine. You should know how to do a bit of research.

From: Sven Lehmann

And what, in your opinion, dear colleague, is the end result of all this supposed to be?

From: Hilke Schneider

Happiness, you dummy! ☺

From: Sven Lehmann

You're the dummy. You've really got a screw loose!

From: Hilke Schneider

So do you! Hey you wanna try that Thai place over by the Magellan terraces? I'm hungry.

From: Sven Lehmann

OK.

From: Hilke Schneider

☺

• • •

At lunch Hilke manages to keep to her half of the deal for just about half an hour. But then she just can't help herself and makes another clumsy but charming attempt to urge Sven to finally "take his happiness into his own hands."

And now Sven doesn't know if he tentatively agreed so that she would finally stop poking her nose into his nonexistent love life or because she had taken the same tack David had. If his buddy weren't so unbelievably blinded by his own infatuation, there's no question he would have advised Sven to write Lilime and politely inform her that she was bothering him and to please cease and desist. But David found the whole text business incredibly fascinating and said things like "Don't be so uptight," "Stay with it!" and "What do you have to lose?"

Whatever the case, it really is time to act. Even Sven is convinced of this by now. If only so that he doesn't lose his mind and risk making his whole sense of well-being dependent on a text message!

Even though his piece still isn't finished yet and it's getting ominously close to press time, Sven takes a crack at composing an answer to all of Lilime's texts. He opens a new Word document

and saves the file in his personal folder under the name "Lilime."
He writes:

> Dear Lilime. I'm sorry for what
> you're going through and I send
> you my deepest sympathies.

Oh God, that sounds like something from a bad movie, Sven thinks.
Without erasing the lines, he just hits the Return key and starts
over again with a new paragraph:

> Dear Lilime. I'm the recipient of all
> your sad messages. Though I am
> deeply moved by your fate, I would
> like to ask you to refrain from sending
> texts to my number. Best regards . . .

Total garbage!
Sven looks out the window. He's happy that Hilke has already
left for the night and he's no longer under close observation.
A new attempt:

> Please refrain from texting this
> number. Respectfully yours . . .

. . . *Mr. Asshole,* thinks Sven.
"This can't possibly be that hard," he exhorts himself, speaking
so loudly that he looks over anxiously at the open door to make
sure none of his coworkers are nearby.

> Dear Lilime, I'm sorry for what you're going through. If you'd like to tell me about your grief in person, rather than just by text, I'd be happy to take you out for coffee. Warm regards, an admirer.

I sound like some creepy guy in his seventies!

> Dear stranger! In case you're curious who's been getting all your moving messages, feel free to get in touch! Sincerely, Your Addressee

Sven stares out the window. How the hell is he supposed to keep from scaring Lilime to death when she gets a text that looks like it's coming from her true love from beyond the grave?

Maybe he should send it from a different cell phone. Unless— could it be that she suspects that her texts are going to some stranger? But then she's sure to be very angry that he's waited so long to write back. No doubt she's just been going on the assumption that the number hasn't been reassigned yet and the texts are all ending up in nirvana.

It's no use. Sven really has to give his job his full attention again. He reaches for his iPhone and types:

> Dear Lilime, I'm the recipient of all your moving words. If I can be of any help to you in your grief, let me know. Your anonymous confidante

Even though Sven just saves this message as a draft for now, rather than sending it off right away, he finally feels more relaxed. The next time he gets in a situation that compels him to act, he'll just send the text off and feel better immediately. But maybe he should wait for a sign.

He shakes his head at this foolish game he's playing in his mind. But at least he can get back to work again now. He takes a deep breath and steels himself for one last effort to finally get the article finished. After all, it's the weekend—he wants to get out of here soon and make it to Tai Chi on time.

· · ·

For the third time tonight, Sven attempts to read the latest text from Lilime. It's almost two o'clock in the morning; the sound of his phone going off must have woken him up. He can barely read the display, which probably has something to do with the bottle of good red wine that he enjoyed on his terrace after Tai Chi. But he absolutely wants to get more information from Lilime's world. Ideally he'll be able to fit it in with the rest and start to understand it right away.

> Thank you for the sign—Beppo's matches! Going to ask him if he'll let me exhibit at his restaurant—I'll order your favorite: Diavola. Promise! Xx, L.

Sven sits up and turns on the light. He reads the text again and wonders if Diavola is a kind of pizza. And if so, how many restaurants could there be in Germany that are owned by someone named Beppo and have that variety of pizza on the menu?

One, ten, or hundreds?

Hard to say. And where do the matches fit in? What kind of sign is Lilime talking about, for God's sake? Does she really believe in that kind of New Agey nonsense?

And what does she want to exhibit, anyway? Her paintings?

I want to see her paintings, Sven thinks, then he gets up to get a bit of fresh air.

It's quite cool on the roof terrace. From here he's got a good view of the few apartments in the surrounding buildings with their lights still on. Across the street he can see a young woman who is sitting in front of the television, wrapped in a towel and painting her toenails. Sven is tempted to go get the telescope he bought for the last partial lunar eclipse. Would it be worth it to take a closer look at this girl?

But he lets this enticing thought go. He would feel sleazy violating his neighbor's privacy like that when she clearly feels safe and secure.

Does Lilime also paint her nails at two o'clock in the morning? Does she even go in for that sort of thing—nails, hair, makeup, and all the rest of it? Do people who have a talent for painting automatically put a lot of stock in appearances?

What kind of paintings does she paint? And does Lilime feel safe and secure when she paints? Wouldn't it be better for him to leave her alone, stay out of her life, give her the space she needs to overcome her grief, and delete whatever texts might come in from now on without reading them?

Sven doesn't care for this thought. It's true he's not thrilled with feeling like a sleazy snoop. But he's even less thrilled at the idea of just staying away from Lilime's world.

He goes to get a bottle of water to help with his post-wine thirst and steps back out onto the terrace. But this time he sits in his beach chair so that he won't be tempted to intrude on his young neighbor with his gaze.

Really though with Lilime it was the other way around, he thinks suddenly and sits up. *She's the one who intruded on me!*

Now he looks up at the starry sky. The Summer Triangle is clearly visible, even though the city is still brightly lit and countless stars remain hidden.

This is a good night to gain some more clarity—Sven can feel it. He goes back into the apartment again, where his MacBook waits in a bag by the door. Itching to get to the bottom of all the mysteries that hang in the air on a special summer night like this one, he grabs the laptop and a hoodie and heads back to the beach chair. Once he's settled he turns the computer on, stares up at the sky while it starts up, and tries to see if he can find Polaris floating above the Big Dipper. When he does finally spot it, it almost feels like it's a sign. Like the one Lilime received. The search will be worth it.

As soon as the little bars in the right-hand corner of the screen indicate that he's online, Sven pulls up Google and starts scouring the vast expanses of the virtual world for Diavola.

clara

Grandma, you make the best mashed potatoes in the world," Clara says with her mouth full. She just loves sitting here with her grandparents and getting to feel like a spoiled little kid again.

"Well, you'd better not let your mother hear you say that!" Lisbeth warns.

Clara groans. Lisbeth likes Clara's mother—but still, they've never really been on the same wavelength, and Clara doesn't quite know how to respond.

But Lisbeth just keeps talking: "You go ahead and eat all you want. I think it's wonderful that you've finally put some weight back on, honey!"

"I have?" Clara asks in amazement and sets her forkful of potatoes back down onto her plate. She glances down at herself.

"Your face isn't so awfully drawn anymore. You're looking really pretty again!" Lisbeth gives Clara a sly look and suddenly breaks into a big grin. "You're not in love, are you?"

"Grandma!" Clara says indignantly. She feels completely blindsided. She has just been happily rhapsodizing about her painting, about how she's finally picked it up again and it's been so much fun—but Lisbeth can't imagine that that might be the reason for her good mood; no, she has to go chalking it up to some imaginary love affair, never mind that the very idea of such a thing is completely ridiculous and unrealistic. *What about Ben? Has everybody forgotten about him already?* Clara asks herself silently.

Lisbeth seems to realize she's gone too far. "You know, sometimes the best way to get over an old love is by finding a new love."

"But maybe I don't want to get over it!" Clara fires back angrily.

"You shouldn't give up hope, though."

"What am I supposed to hope for? Things aren't ever going to be good again; it's never going to be like it used to be."

"And nobody is saying it will be, honey. But you can try to make the best of the situation."

They both go silent. Clara crosses her arms over her chest defensively.

"Honey, you're a young, beautiful woman and talented, too, and—"

"And intelligent!" Willy interjects, smiling proudly as he pushes his plate toward the gravy boat so that Lisbeth can top him up.

"But do you think Ben would want for you to be alone?" Lisbeth asks gently—though it sounds pretty damn harsh.

"Oh, leave the kid alone and let her eat," her grandfather says.

"It's okay," Clara responds. "I know you two mean well. But why don't you tell me what was so urgent?"

Clara had barely made it through the door when Lisbeth started talking excitedly, saying she had big news.

It turns out that Lisbeth has inherited a "big pile" of money from her aunt, even though they'd only been in touch sporadically for years.

"She was ninety-seven. An impressive age," Willy declares, "and Lisbeth is her only living relative."

"Now of course we don't actually know yet how much money it is or how much the funeral is going to cost," Lisbeth adds. "I've asked your uncle to make the arrangements."

After lunch, when, as usual, Willy goes to the living room to take a little nap in his armchair, Clara starts shifting around restlessly in her chair. Finally she leans forward a little.

"Lisbeth?" she begins carefully. The look on her grandma's face makes it plain that she knows something's coming—it must be important if her granddaughter is calling her by her first name. "Do you believe in signs?"

Lisbeth leans back and clears her throat. "What kind of signs do you mean?"

"I don't know, just, signs—from up there." Clara gestures with her head up toward the ceiling.

"You mean, like, if the sun shines tomorrow, we're going to inherit some money soon?"

"Yeah, something like that. I mean, I think . . ." Clara hesitates. "I think Ben is sending me signs." She looks at Lisbeth expectantly, puts her hands under her chin, props herself up on the table with her elbows, and adds: "Silly, huh?"

"That is not at all silly."

"It's not?"

"Quite the opposite. It's smart. You know, honey, when your dear father left us all those years ago, I did a lot of thinking about life and the way things are and how it's hard sometimes to see the reason behind things. And I came to the conclusion that it pays to believe in something."

"Uh-huh. That's too abstract for me."

"When fate deals people a blow, they either lose their faith, or they find their way to God or some kind of religion for the first time."

"But Grandma, I'm not talking about God, I'm talking about Ben. The signs are from him!"

"What kind of signs are they—do you mind telling me?"

"Well, like last night for example. I had just finished a large canvas, and I was sitting there; I'd poured myself a glass of wine and I was thinking about what I should do with all these paintings, whether there might be a way to exhibit them somewhere or even sell them. So anyway, I thought I'd light a few candles, and I went over to the cupboard to look for a lighter. But I couldn't find one, so I went to the living room and started rummaging through a few drawers. Finally I was about to give up and was trying to shut the last drawer when it got stuck. I had to take everything out to check which of the papers or whatever else might have gotten stuck back there. It was this matchbook."

Clara reaches into her back pocket, pulls out a little matchbook, and places it on the table.

Lisbeth picks it up and studies the writing on the cover. She gives Clara a somewhat puzzled look.

"Castello?"

"It's the Italian place that Ben and I always went to. And yesterday it suddenly occurred to me: Beppo, I mean the guy who owns the place, exhibits paintings and photographs every now and then. With little price tags with big numbers on them. So then I thought . . . well, maybe I can show him my paintings sometime, too. It's just an idea . . . But even if it sounds totally ridiculous, it feels like Ben sent me this sign. Do you understand?"

Clara looks at her grandma, waiting for an answer. Lisbeth smiles contentedly and sits there in silence.

"Well? You're not saying anything!" Clara says with frustration.

"I don't really need to say anything. Some things in life are meaningful enough just the way they are. You don't have to go looking for an explanation for them or dress them up in words."

"Oh, Grandma, I just get scared sometimes. I feel like I'm going nuts. You don't think I've gone off the deep end?"

"Not at all," says Lisbeth, and seeing the desperate look on her granddaughter's face she puts her hand on her shoulder. "You know, the question isn't if there are such things as signs or not. The question is whether you choose to see them that way, and how you choose to interpret them."

Clara gives her grandmother a skeptical look.

"Every positive thought is going to help you to get through this incredibly difficult time in your life and make things a little easier. Everything that strengthens your faith in the good in this world is just incredibly important for you, especially now. Faith in goodness and faith in love!"

Lisbeth gets up out of her chair and leans over Clara, who sits there confused and waits for whatever else her grandmother might have to say.

"Honey, you have two options: Either you believe in goodness and the unexplainable, or you don't. Think hard about which makes you feel better!" Now Lisbeth raises her eyebrows and nods, signaling to Clara that it's her turn to speak.

Clara hesitates. After a brief silence she says: "You're right. All this suffering just has to have some deeper purpose. I want to believe in the good in this world. Otherwise I'd just have to give up."

sven

All right, listen, I need your help."

"Good morning to you, too. Why yes, thank you, I did have a nice weekend. How sweet of you to ask," Hilke teases her colleague, shaking her head sarcastically as she walks into the office in a rush. "What's up? Trouble with Breiding?"

"No, new info from Lilime." Sven doesn't know whether to look forward to Hilke's reaction or dread it.

"What? Really?" Hilke cries. She suddenly looks wide awake. "Well, come on, out with it. What happened?"

"Nothing."

"Oooooh, you're driving me nuts. Why is it always like pulling teeth trying to get you to tell me something?"

"I just did a little research because I was bored."

"And?"

"That's it. There wasn't a whole lot I could turn up. I only know that she apparently lives in a city with an Italian restaurant that's owned by someone named Beppo and has a type of pizza on its menu called Diavola."

"Oh, yum."

"You've heard of it?"

"Yeah, super-delicious, really spicy, and flavorful. It's Martin's favorite kind of pizza."

"It's Lilime's lost love's favorite, too."

"Okay, and what else?" asks Hilke, who is still staring at him eagerly across the desk.

"That's it—nothing else. According to the internet there are forty-five restaurants in forty different cities in Germany owned by someone named Giuseppe. And I know that at least three of these have a Pizza Diavola on the menu."

"Why Giuseppe? Oh right, from Beppo, got it. And what else besides that?"

"Nothing!"

"Well, what about Hamburg? Is Hamburg one of the cities? I think there's a Giuseppe who works at the pizzeria around the corner from us."

"You see? That just proves how low the chances are of tracking down this one Italian guy out of the hundreds of Giuseppes out there, not to mention how hard it would be to identify Lilime even if I did."

Hilke drops onto her chair. She's silent for a moment. "Okay, Sven, be honest now. Why don't you just call her?" she asks, wearing that typical smug grin of hers.

Sven grimaces and rolls his eyes.

"Fine, not a good idea. But what if *I* call her again? Under a different pretext?" Hilke has an innocent look on her face, like a child who's hatching some scheme.

"No. That's dumb. What are you going to say to her? That you've dialed the wrong number again, but you would still like to know her name?"

"I could also call and just hang up as soon as she answers. She might say her name right when she picks up."

"All she says when she picks up is 'Hello.' It—"

"Oh, no way!!! So now you finally admit it. You've totally spoken to her! And you want me to think you're not one bit interested in her . . . the nerve!"

"I have not spoken to her!" Sven has to think fast—how is he going to get himself out of this one? "But this is definitely the kind of person who only ever answers with 'Hello' or 'Yes?'"

"Well, I'd say it is worth a try. What's the number again?"

Sven reads off Lilime's number—half reluctant, half excited to see if anything useful comes out of this juvenile, half-baked scheme.

But Hilke already has the receiver pressed to her ear and is dialing the number. "Oh God, I'm so nervous! It's ringing!" she whispers conspiratorially.

"I know," Sven says, amused—he can't help knowing; his colleague put it on speaker.

"Yes?" The sound fills the room.

"Um, South German Lottery, good day, Ms. . . . uh, am I speaking with . . . ," Hilke glances at Sven, pleading for help. She looks pretty out of her depth; Sven immediately feels embarrassed for her. If he could he would run out of the room. But there's clearly no going back now. He gestures with a shrug at the poster hanging on the closed door—a cartoon showing Angela Merkel and Condoleezza Rice testing each other's strength in an arm-wrestling match.

Hilke continues: "Am I speaking with Rice, er, Reis, Cornelia Reis?"

"No," the voice on the other end of the line answers politely.

"I have some good news for you. You have been selected from a pool of five hundred candidates to take part in our free sweepstakes—"

"Not interested!" the voice interrupts, sounding a bit annoyed now. "My name's not Reis and I'm not dumb enough to get involved in this silly nonsense. You must have the wrong number."

"My apologies, Ms. . . . uh, what is your name, if I may ask?"

"No, you may not ask!"

"Fair enough. It would be in your interest though to let us update your information, because then you would be able to participate in our complimentary, zero-obligation—"

The voice, getting louder now, interrupts Hilke again.

"How can you sleep at night knowing you have such an obnoxious job? If I were in your shoes, I'd rather clean floors for a living! I'm hanging up now!"

Hilke's face is beet red. She stares at the receiver, stunned, as if it might hold some clue to what just happened.

Sven leans back in his chair with a big grin on his face, folds his hands behind his head, and says smugly: "Now that's what I call a successful interview. We should have gotten our interns in here to watch!"

Hilke makes a vague sound then shoots Sven a furious look.

"I don't know what your deal is! Now we know at least that Lilime's name isn't Cornelia, that she probably doesn't work at a call center, and on top of that that she's neither gullible nor dimwitted." Hilke grins proudly.

"Yeah, crazy!" Sven fires back. "I have to get to the conference room. I'll be sure to tell everyone about your innovative new research technique."

Hilke grabs her mouse pad and flings it at Sven. She doesn't even come close to hitting him, though, and he just grins back silently.

Sven walks out shaking his head. He badly needs some fresh air and decides to go for a walk along the Elbe after the meeting.

. . .

A few days later, a giant ship is visible on the horizon. Sven is surprised, because he didn't see anything in the papers today about this huge rust bucket docking in the harbor.

Then again, he hasn't been reading the obligatory daily papers with particular care of late. He should be conscientiously poring over the leading news sources and checking all the international business papers for tips on new topics, but all he wants to do is scan the culture pages and the classifieds for art exhibitions and Italian restaurants, anything that might lead him to Lilime. Even here, walking along the Grosse Elbstrasse, he catches himself scanning every storefront for signs of Italian cuisine.

Some days, when he's out running, he'll even go out of his way or slow down to get a better look. Whenever he does this it throws off his rhythm and he ends up mad at himself afterward because he can no longer objectively measure whether or not he's improved his time on his six-mile route. It's all too clear to him how much he's neglected his training. He's fallen way behind, especially when it comes to swimming. Between now and next spring, when he plans to compete in his first triathlon, he'll need a lot of sessions at the pool.

But by this point the case of the mysterious Lilime has become something like a real hobby. It's like a detective game or a logic exercise, where with the help of some clever reasoning you narrow the options down till you're left with only one possible solution.

This week, though, there hasn't been much in the way of clues. Somebody named Niklas is really into Lilime's paintings and something's going on that has her thinking about going freelance out of necessity—that's all Sven has learned from the two texts he's received in the past few days, and nothing aside from that.

As the ship gets closer, Sven starts thinking about what kind of work Lilime might do. If she's thinking about setting out on her own and doing something with painting, that could mean she studied art or works as a teacher. But what teacher would willingly give up the security and benefits that come with a government job? Maybe one who is totally unloved and harassed by colleagues and students alike because she wears weird wool skirts and reeks of sweat.

Sven winces. No, that doesn't seem like her. He can't really explain it, but he gets the feeling that Lilime is the exact opposite of boring or unattractive. Her texts convey so much sensitivity and liveliness. She must have a rich, well-rounded personality. No doubt she's really pretty and at an age where, sure, she's invested a fair amount into her career, but on the other hand she's still got enough spark left to finally realize her potential and start doing her own thing.

If the situation that's forcing her to act is market related, then that would mean she's bound to work for some company on a salary basis. Something hip, like maybe she does layout at a publishing house or comes up with designs for a fashion company.

Suddenly Sven is reminded of a good friend of Fiona's. A while ago she'd asked him for some tax advice because she wanted to start her own studio. The company she worked for had gone bankrupt, so she was now unemployed and was trying to start her own business with the help of start-up subsidies from the employment office.

At the time Sven wasn't able to do more than give her a few names of people she could get in touch with. But through her story he had hit upon a trend of lots of young and highly qualified people making a virtue of necessity and daring to make the leap into working freelance or starting their own businesses. Sven had done some research and compiled a ton of data on the subject, which met with quick approval at the editorial meeting. Breiding wanted to make a big thing of it. But then other topics had taken priority. Now, though, Sven thinks, in light of the global financial crisis, he could dust the idea off and propose it again.

Maybe he could also use it as a way to get in touch with Lilime. He could interview her or write a profile on her, presenting her as someone who was representative of a large number of workers.

Sven quickens his pace a little. The ship is only about a quarter mile away at this point.

That's it, thinks Sven. *That's how I'll meet Lilime!* Now he has a legit and completely innocent reason to get in touch with her!

Suddenly the ship's horn blares, loud and deep, and Sven is jolted out of his reverie. As if an alarm clock had gone off, he turns around and starts heading back to the office, taking long strides as he walks along the Elbe.

clara

What a shitty Friday! And it had gotten off to such a good start.

Furious, Clara stares out the window of her office, not looking at anything in particular. Niklas can be such a giant asshole! Inside Clara is seething with rage, and she's glad that Antje isn't at her desk at the moment. She mustn't let anything show for now. Everyone else will learn the dire news soon enough. She would never have thought that the agency was in such bad shape.

What am I supposed to do now? Clara asks herself softly. A thousand thoughts are running through her head all at once. Maybe she should have just taken that ridiculous call from the shameless lottery lady as a sign and gone for broke! After all, she's going to need all the money she can get soon enough.

"Try to look at this as a positive thing, Clara. You have so much potential. Use it!" Her boss's words are still ringing in her ears. The thing is, what pisses Clara off isn't what Niklas was trying to tell her—it was the way he went about it.

He'd tried to act all sweet as he told her she was being laid off and to pitch the whole thing as if it were a piece of sensationally good news.

If only I'd never shown him the photos of my paintings, thinks Clara, and she sinks back in her desk chair. She's been staring at her monitor for hours now. The screensaver shows images of cosmic objects, alternating one after another—stars, Mars, the moon.

She just has to talk to someone.

Katja!

Clara speed-dials Katja's number and hopes that Antje doesn't come back to their shared office all too soon.

"Hey, babe! What's up?"

"Did I wake you up? You sound so quiet."

"No, I'm at a conference," whispers Katja.

"Oh, shit. Well, just give me a call back later."

"No, it's okay. It's totally boring anyway. I just can't leave or else I'll draw attention to myself. But I can listen, I've got my earbuds in. So go ahead, shoot!"

"Okay, I'll try to make it quick: I'm going to be out of a job soon!"

"What?" Katja cries so loudly that her cover is sure to be blown. "Sorry," Clara hears her friend saying. "Yes, I know this is a conference. But this is an emergency!"

"Oh God," says Clara.

"'Oh God' is right!" Katja says, lowering her voice again. "So what happened?"

"Niklas suggested that I leave. Our main competition outpitched us and lured away one of our most important clients."

"Shit," whispers Katja. "So what now?"

"No idea. I guess I'll go clean floors . . ."

"Ugh, babe. Don't talk like that. Everybody knows how great

you are. Niklas just wants to get rid of you because you're his highest-paid employee—which is criminal, by the way, with that joke they call your salary and all the unpaid overtime you put in." Katja is beginning to sound suspiciously loud again.

"Yeah, but I believe him when he says he doesn't have a choice. And he's just putting it out there for now. I mean, I've been here longer than anyone else. For that reason alone he wouldn't just send me packing to balance the payroll—only if I see it as an opportunity."

"Was that *his* neat little way of putting it?"

"Well, I mean, I showed Niklas my paintings the other day. And he says I should do more with my talent than just sit at a computer all day."

"Mmm, well, I've long been of the opinion that you should finally get yourself out of that snoozefest of a company. Will you be home tonight? I'll come by and we'll do some brainstorming, okay? Right now though I've gotta go. I'm not exactly making any friends here . . ."

"Yes, I'll be home. Thanks, Katja. See you tonight!" Clara says, somewhat relieved, and realizes with surprise that she's been whispering this whole time, too.

• • •

Clara's hands are shaking as she walks into Beppo's restaurant that night. She tried to talk Katja out of this idea, but her friend said it was time to stop avoiding the places she'd gone to in the past.

But maybe this feeling of uneasiness is simply due to the fact that she hasn't been here in what feels like an eternity. She's afraid of seeing something that will plunge her back in a deep hole and erase all the progress she's made recently.

The blow she was dealt today was huge. Suddenly she's looking at the prospect of being without a steady income, and the very thought of it has her so distressed that she's afraid that the tender new courage to face life that she's felt in the past few weeks could give way to another bout of depression. But maybe some of Katja's energy and optimism will rub off on her.

Her friend is late again—typical—leaving Clara to read the menu front and back over and over again, even though she has zero appetite.

How many times had she and Ben sat here sharing a plate of antipasti? They'd always fought over the one piece of pepperoni in the middle—only to share it in the end, fair and square. Usually Clara was so full after that that Ben had to scarf down both entrées by himself.

Maybe Grandma and Katja really are right, thinks Clara as she keeps impatiently glancing over at the entrance. Somehow she has to try to make the best of things. Even if she's never going to sit at this table with Ben again, she still has to try to keep all the familiar objects, moments, and places in her heart—like Beppo's restaurant. She should create new memories that don't hurt, memories that feel good. She has to have new experiences that are positive, so that her head can stop constantly dividing her life into a Before and After.

Just as Beppo is stopping by again to ask if there's anything he can do or bring for her while she waits, Katja comes rushing through the door.

"Sorry, babe. I was just in the car this whole time stuck on a phone call."

"With a young, handsome man, eh?!" Beppo asks playfully,

and without actually waiting for an answer he marches back off to the kitchen.

Katja stares after him, confused, then she's finally there for Clara.

After two bottles of prosecco Katja's love life and Clara's prospects of a professional rebirth are looking quite a bit rosier.

Beppo, too, proves happy to have the opportunity to help Clara out. Right there on the spot he offers to let her exhibit her paintings at the restaurant—its walls are hers, he says; she may do with them what she pleases.

"Bella!" Beppo cries out with delight as he clears the plates. "Even if you just made scribbles, I'd do anything for you. But your paintings are magnificent, darling. My customers are gonna love you!"

Clara shows him a few photos of her moon series on her phone. After seeing them he grabs her thin and deeply bewildered-looking face with both hands, kisses her on both cheeks, and declares: "Bambina, I'm excited. You're such a fine girl. I believe in you."

Then he waves Clara and Katja over to join him at his table and sample a freshly prepared dish of crème brûlée.

When Clara gets back home she feels like she's going to burst. But still she's so happy and motivated by all the encouragement from Katja and Beppo that she feels like she could get right to work.

As she's thinking about it, she also adds Ben to her group of supporters and starts putting together a long list in her head. *What are all the things I still want to achieve in my life?* she asks herself. *What have I always wanted to try? When I get to the end of my life, what projects will I regret not having at least tried to make happen?*

Clara makes herself a cup of tea and reflects. For so many years now she has dreamed of developing a painting style that's unmistakably her own. She wants to move people with her art, to speak to them; she wants to make the kind of work that people would want to hang in their living room. Whenever she lines up the canvases in the long hallway and silently takes in the impression they make on her, Clara is filled with an incredible feeling of happiness. At such moments, everything else around her is unimportant and far away. She is at peace with herself and the world.

Maybe she should think seriously about a career as a painter? Clara senses a lot of positive energy all of a sudden.

My moon paintings are just the beginning, she thinks. I can feel it!

Now all of a sudden even her worries about financial security start to seem very small. She just can't wait to make all her new ideas a reality. But would she really be able to support herself by selling paintings? From exhibiting and doing commission work?

Niklas assured her that she could keep working for him on a freelance basis for a while, which would help her avoid a sudden drop-off in income. She would also be able to keep using the agency's offices for a while after she left. Niklas seemed already to have done a lot of thinking about how he could best help to make the transition easier for her. And if he actually meant his offer in earnest, Clara could save a lot of money on printing costs for business cards and mailers, establishing a web presence, and other promotional steps.

She already has her first official commission: Tonight Beppo ordered a handful of watercolors of Lüneburg scenes that he can present to his customers as surprise gifts.

This in turn gave Katja the idea of Clara offering to do affordably priced commission work on an individual basis. She said that the market for tasteful nude photographs of pregnant women and new couples was booming. So maybe it could work with paintings, too.

Clara thinks: *If I approach this the right way and manage to make a name for myself, at least in the Lüneburg and Hamburg area, I might even be able to fill a very specialized niche in the market.* Plus she could also go looking for customers on the internet. The customer sends a photo over email, and just like that she's got something on which to base a portrait, a nude, or some other personalized gift.

Katja had also suggested that she start building her network and really make an effort to reach out to people with similar interests on local networking sites like XING. She herself had been able to drum up a lot of work through such connections. More than that, by the time they were on the second bottle of prosecco Katja was almost bursting with excitement as the idea suddenly came to her of also offering her own clients an expanded portfolio. Sure, she could expand her standard package of services as an interior designer to include specific recommendations of ways her clients could use a few color accents to add a very personal and unique note to their space—for example by displaying Clara's individually crafted works of art. Naturally Katja had immediately developed the idea further, which is to say she started thinking about all the great things they could do with the extra income. But then Clara did feel obliged to dampen her euphoria a bit. After all, she can't take on everything at once; first she needs a well-thought-out plan for getting started as a freelance artist and graphic designer.

For that reason the first thing on the docket now is to take a thorough inventory of what material she has on hand. Clara has a feeling that she has a massive reorganization effort ahead of her. When she and Ben moved into this apartment, she'd had to stick all her boxes and paintings way in the back of the long, narrow storage space in the basement. She never imagined that there would ever be a reason for needing to access them more frequently than their tools, flower pots, or spare bike parts.

And all of a sudden curiosity takes hold of her. It's late, sure, but why not go down there right now?

Clara grabs her sweater and the key to the basement and marches off down the stairs.

But when she steps into the somewhat musty storage room, she suddenly feels a sharp pain in her chest. There's Ben's bike. *Well, of course*, she thinks, trying to calm herself down; *it's not like it was going to just vanish into thin air.* He had ridden it all over Lüneburg and the surrounding countryside—and he'd been riding it even more often in the time just before his death. Only now does it occur to Clara that maybe he had had to leave her car behind so often in the last few months of his life because he was using drugs more frequently than ever before.

Clara had also forgotten the basketball—here it is rolling up to her feet. Ben might have been one of the shortest players on his club team, but he could jump higher than any of them.

After music, basketball was his biggest hobby. But about a year after they met, he suddenly stopped wanting to go to practice. Today this decision of his also appears in a new light. At the time Ben just claimed that he couldn't get along with the new coach.

Clara looks down at all the other objects that suddenly catapult her back into the past and asks herself if it's at all possible to look back objectively. Dr. Ferdinand has tried to get her to understand that the best she can do is to try to come up with her own version of the truth about what really happened to Ben. But even if she were to come up with one—what is it supposed to look like?

Is suicide worse than an accident? Or is it the other way around? If someone chooses to kill himself as a way of escaping an unbearable life, is that less tragic than if he dies without choosing to, solely as the result of some unbearable combination of random circumstances?

Clara sinks to a crouch on the floor and buries her face in her hands.

She doesn't want to cry. She wants to finally get out of the darkness. She wants to go into the light.

She wants her colorful past back—and that means she now has to figure out the quickest way to get to her canvasses.

Since not a single one of the boxes is labeled, she doesn't have much of a choice other than to take a quick look inside each of them. But it's mostly just old dishes and old junk—nobody could possibly have any use for this stuff. Same goes for this box filled with who knows how many cables—Clara doesn't even begin to know what Ben might have wanted to do with it. She decides to take it upstairs with her and give it to Knut when she has the chance in the hopes that the guys find the courage to keep their band going somehow.

After another quarter of an hour she has succeeded in reaching a canvas wrapped in an old bedsheet. She pulls off the covering— and even in the faint light of the cellar, a wonderfully radiant red has Clara beaming. She picks the painting up. Giant poppies are visible on the canvas; she had been smitten with them during one of the many vacations on the Baltic that she took with her grandparents as a child. With just a few, broad strokes she had hinted at the flowers' shape. Immediately they take Clara back to a time when everything was more colorful.

sven

For several days now there hasn't been a single sign of life from Lilime. And Sven's impatience is starting to manifest itself in a blind urge to act. Or at least that's Hilke's smug take on it, which she delivers, naturally, with a big grin on her face.

By this point he has scoped out nine Hamburg neighborhoods on his bike in the vague hope that chance would put him on Lilime's trail. Sure, he tries to tell himself that these extra rides and detours are just additional training for his triathlon, but deep down he knows full well that he would go to almost any length, however futile, in order to find this mysterious stranger.

But why should Lilime live in Hamburg, anyway? She could just as well live in any other city or town in Germany, Sven thinks with a sigh.

Whenever an opportunity has presented itself in the last few days, Sven has searched the web for anything that might lead him to exhibitions of moon paintings. He's even started looking on eBay for paintings that meet this description.

But so far all his efforts have been in vain. He's even canvassed countless Italian joints—none of them have gotten him any further.

David, who like Hilke continues to follow the story with interest, urges him to just call Lilime straight out. He should just say he's a journalist and ask her for an interview. All he had to do when he called was claim that he'd heard she was trying to go freelance. And if he were to cleverly alert her to the fact that the article would basically be free publicity and would have an incalculable promotional effect, nothing could go wrong. He just had to sound serious enough when he made his request.

If only it were that simple, Sven thinks, then he turns off the reading lamp in his living room. He stares thoughtfully into the darkness. The rain is pounding hard against the large windows and the flat roof, and the whole loft is filled with a wonderful sound.

His reflection appears in the windowpane, and Sven sits studying his face for a long time. He looks tired. But he likes the stubble that he's let grow for a few days; it seems to make a more mature man of him.

Suddenly he sits up. *If Lilime doesn't write by Sunday, I will actually take matters into my own hands and just call her,* he decides. He looks at his reflection and grins.

clara

After a long walk in the park, Clara is now sitting on a bench by the river and looking wearily out over the water. In her hand she holds an orange envelope. Before her the Ilmenau flows peacefully along. From here it continues on its course, running past the medieval buildings of Lüneburg's busy city center and finally flowing into the Elbe.

Just a few months ago, when Clara stood on the harbor in Hamburg with Dorothea and stared out over the gray water, Ben's death was still shrouded in mystery. Only today does she finally seem to have arrived at a comforting and at the same time painful clarity—clarity over the fact that Ben probably fell from that balcony on purpose.

For the past few days, Clara has only been functioning in the most basic mechanical sense, in a way that's similar to how she acted in the time between when she first received news of his death and the funeral. The initial euphoria that she felt in planning her career as a painter was immediately wiped away when she found the thick folder in the box of music gear. The word "Private" was written on the cover in large letters, and below it the words "Please DO NOT read!"

At first Clara was hesitant to open the folder, unsure whether the secrecy was just a bit of childishness or if Ben truly meant that the contents were nobody's concern but his. She asked herself whether she or Ben's family had a natural right to obtain information from his inner life.

But that same night she worked up her nerve, opened the clasp with trembling hands, and spread the contents out on her bed. What she found were diary-like pieces of writing, a few photos and song lyrics of Ben's, plus old photos and postcards. Even after a brief glance through the items, Clara understood what kind of documents she was looking at. Judging from the dates she could see that this material bore witness to several years of Ben's life. It was instantly clear to her that she wouldn't be able to ignore his request. On the other hand, however, she was incapable of disregarding Ben's injunction not to read what was in this folder. She couldn't go behind his back. Wouldn't Ben have wanted his wishes to be respected? Wouldn't that have been more important to him than any other consideration?

But more than anything, Clara was terribly afraid of finding out something that would disturb her. For a moment she considered if maybe Katja or Dorothea . . . ? But she felt it wouldn't be right.

That night Clara spent hours tossing and turning in bed. It wasn't until the early morning hours that she decided that the best thing would be to entrust the folder to a person who hadn't known Ben. It would have to be someone who would read the material conscientiously and was in a position to judge whether the writings could really be of any comfort to Ben's loved ones. In this way she would be acting at least partially in accordance with what Ben wanted.

And all at once the solution to this problem seemed close at hand. First thing in the morning Clara called her therapist to ask if she would be willing to look through the folder for insights into Ben's state of mind. Politely but firmly, Dr. Ferdinand asked for a day to think about it, but then she called back that same afternoon to say that she thought Clara's idea was a good one and made sense.

After Clara had dropped the folder off at the therapist's office she was at first relieved not to have its contents lurking around her apartment anymore. But the following night she slept just as restlessly. Clara could hardly wait to find out what Dr. Ferdinand would say, even though she was terrified of what she might learn. She kept speculating over and over again about what the writings might reveal about Ben's mental and emotional state.

The next morning Clara got a call from Dr. Ferdinand asking her to come see her at her office. Clara let Antje know that she'd be a bit late coming into work and headed out.

With knees trembling she stepped into Dr. Ferdinand's office, which on every other occasion but this one always seemed like a warm and safe space. Dr. Ferdinand offered Clara some tea like she did at all her other sessions and asked her to sit. In her hand she held an orange envelope with no writing on it which had caught Clara's eye when she'd first looked through Ben's folder herself.

Dr. Ferdinand placed the envelope on the small, low table between them and said with a gentle smile: "This letter is for you. Now, bear in mind, it was over a year ago that your boyfriend wrote it. But still, it might contain a few answers to your questions."

Clara felt like she couldn't breathe. She didn't know what she was supposed to feel or think, much less say.

"It's a farewell letter," Dr. Ferdinand continued. "And even if Ben didn't leave it to you directly, I still think you should read it."

"So it says in there that he wanted to kill himself?" Clara asked in a thick voice.

"Not directly. But I think we can now assume that he didn't want this life. There are many other indications in his writings that point to what I already suspected. Whether it was ultimately an accident caused by too much drug use or if he intentionally jumped—your boyfriend was clearly searching, in vain, for ways to bring his dark side in harmony with his radiant side."

Clara swallowed hard. She felt the tears welling up inside her.

"Ms. Sommerfeld, I suggest you keep this letter for yourself and hand all the other documents over to his family. That way they can decide for themselves what they'd like to do with them. You don't have to bear the responsibility for this all on your own."

• • •

Even now, sitting on the bench by the river, these words are still echoing in Clara's head. She stares out at the water as if in a trance. She can't stop thinking of the dreadful fight that she and Ben had the last night she saw him alive. Of how she told him she thought he was incapable of taking on any responsibility and criticized him for not being in control of his life. Even if she deeply regrets everything she said, a mute reproach would probably have driven him just as far from her sooner or later. She was simply too weak to counteract the strength of the dark world he inhabited.

She's still holding Ben's farewell letter in her hands. On a sudden impulse, she now decides to finally open it.

With trembling fingers she pulls a letter handwritten on a white sheet of paper out of the envelope and starts to read:

>*Dear Clara,*
>
>*When you read this, I'll be gone, and I'm sorry that I'm too much of a coward to tell you the truth to your face.*
>
>*The truth is that ever since I was fifteen years old the only thing I ever think about is when's the next time I can get high. I go from one bender to the next, and in between there's just this buzzing in my head that I can't bear anymore.*
>
>*I don't want to drag you down any further into my screwed-up life. And you shouldn't think any higher of me than I do myself. I hate myself. I hate myself for everything, but above all for not being able to love you the way you deserve to be loved.*
>
>*Follow your own path. Mine's a dead end.*
>
>*Take care of yourself, you hear me!*
>
>>*Ben*

Clara cries. She doesn't sob; she just cries, silently and for a long time. Finally she takes several deep breaths, in and out. Then she takes a brief glance up at the overcast sky and folds the letter to make a little paper boat.

She knows she will keep Ben's words in her heart. But she wants to be rid of this letter, this letter that proves beyond a doubt just how little she knew the man she was going to marry and how brittle the foundation on which their love rested really must have been.

Clara walks a few steps down to the riverbank, takes her ring off her finger, kisses it gently, and places it on the pointed top of the little boat. Carefully she puts the paper in the water. At first it threatens to tip over to one side and sink, but then it makes a little turn, rights itself, and the water carries it on ahead. Bobbing jerkily up and down, it finally finds its way downriver.

Clara watches the white speck as it goes, eyes blurry with tears. Just as the little boat turns around a bend in the river and disappears, a small gap suddenly opens up in the clouds and the sun breaks through.

On this late afternoon that Clara thought would remain gloomy and dim, a few rays of sunlight finally make it through the gray sheet of clouds. With a meek smile and shaky knees, Clara sets off for home.

sven

As he's crossing the bridges over the Elbe headed south, Sven surprises himself by letting out a quick laugh. He still can't believe that he actually took off work early and asked Hilke to lend him her car.

"Lüneburg! I'm almost positive it's Lüneburg!" It was with these words that he greeted his colleague when he came into the office that morning. Excited as a little boy, he told her about the latest text from Lilime.

"Her real name is actually Clara. Clara with a C. So probably the same Clara that Theo was going to look after."

Hilke flashed him a cheeky grin and promptly accused him of falling head over heels for a stranger and of being jealous to boot—all of which he happily ignored. He didn't care if she made fun of him. The only thing he was interested in was whether Hilke was willing to do without her car for an evening.

Naturally she would have preferred to come along herself, but she and her husband had been invited to her mother-in-law's house tonight. Sven is glad to be able to conduct his search in peace, without Hilke spoiling everything with her annoying commentary.

And now he's on his way to Lüneburg to search for Lilime. The fact that the chariot conveying him to the stranger he seeks had to be an old, embarrassing Opel does put a bit of a damper on his teenager-like enthusiasm, true. But ever since he got the text yesterday, he's been downright obsessed with giving in to his intuition and just doing something totally crazy for once. Something that feels like living—something he never would have thought he was even capable of before tonight.

For a brief moment he looks out at the glittering water and is immediately reminded of the words Clara wrote. Even though the message moved him just as much as most of the others before it, this last one was different. It sounded like the same Lilime, full of naive longing and corny words, but at the same time he could hear Clara speaking, and she seemed in every way to be the mature and sophisticated person whom Sven had always guessed was behind Lilime.

Even the time that the text arrived was new. Just as Sven was working on what he was going to say when he called, trying to get it just right, his phone dinged—for days he had hardly let it out of his sight.

Sven still doesn't actually have a plan for what to do next, but he's optimistic that he's getting at least a little bit closer to Clara.

And to think that this whole time she's been much closer than he would ever have dared to hope!

Lüneburg is no more than thirty miles away from Hamburg, and Sven is wondering to himself why he's never spent any time in this little medieval city, not counting a school field trip he went on as a kid. If nothing else, Lüneburg of all places apparently boasts the most bars per capita in all of Europe. At least that's what came up while Sven was researching today, searching the internet to try to find all the Italian restaurants in town that exhibited paintings.

Driving along on the A250 now, he pictures himself going up to a young woman on the street and asking if she knows of a good Italian restaurant. In his imagination, she would decide right there on the spot to join him for dinner and finally would turn out to be Clara.

Sven has to grin at this silly fantasy. He turns the radio up as loud as it will go, never mind that he doesn't even like the song that's playing. Hilke's pitiful CD collection is just as boring; it doesn't offer much more than musical soundtracks and shallow soft rock. But tonight it doesn't bother him. Tonight everything is different. He could run a marathon in under three hours, that's how energized he feels.

But as Sven passes the town of Winsen, the doubts start to creep in—maybe it would be wiser to give up and head back home. What happens if his search today is successful and all of a sudden he's really standing before the real Clara? What is he actually supposed to say? Will he even like her? What if she's both dumb and dumb-looking? Or even worse: What if Clara is such a beautiful vision of a woman that he can't think of a single sensible thing to say that doesn't sound too much like a crude come-on?

He keeps going through many more possibilities in his head, and meanwhile the time passes so quickly that he's downright startled to see a sign all of a sudden that reads "Lüneburg North." He follows the signs that lead him toward the city center until he comes to a red light and has to stop. Sven hesitates. Should he take this as an omen and turn back right now?

But when the light turns green his foot hits the gas pedal; it's almost like he's in a trance. Not five minutes later he finds a parking space on a little square right next to the pedestrian zone. Before he gets out he looks down at his phone's display to read Clara's text one more time.

> Oh Ben, I'm so incredibly sorry that I couldn't help you. If there's even anything to forgive, then I forgive you. And I promise you I'll take care of myself as best I can. The Ilmenau has carried your letter away, but I'll carry you in my heart forever. Clara

The words move him. *Will Clara be able to forgive me, too?* Sven wonders. *After all, I'm literally spying on her.*

He takes a deep breath, then he gets out of the car and marches off.

clara

"This one! This one just has to be part of the show!" Karin says proudly. Her eyes are almost shining as she lifts up the square canvas that shows a beach scene in Hohwacht in harsh, alienating colors.

Clara doesn't particularly like this painting. She painted it when she was feeling, yet again, like she'd been abandoned by her mother and was thinking back on that vacation on the Baltic. True, she had always enjoyed the walks that she, Lisbeth, and Willy took, but nevertheless, every day of that vacation there were unvoiced reproaches and accusations hanging in the air.

Her grandmother never saying a word, but expressing with her looks and gestures how little she understood her daughter in law. And her grandfather, behind closed doors in the bedroom of the rental apartment, lamenting in a whisper to Lisbeth, wondering aloud why Karin so often left her daughter to fend for herself when she was still so little and needed her mother more than ever.

Now would really be a good opportunity to finally have it out with my mother, thinks Clara as she stares absently at the painting. But ever since Ben's letter turned up she just hasn't had the energy for anything—and definitely not for an argument.

Even though the summer weather has proved to be especially pleasant in the past few weeks, Clara feels like it's the worst time of the year, as when winter fills her with a sense of melancholy and she fears, this time, it won't ever disappear.

"Hey, what's going on with you?" her mother asks suddenly, and to Clara's ears it sounds like an affront. She'd really like to just let it all out: My boyfriend is dead, my mother is heartless, I'm about to be out of a job, and I'm never going to find a man who I can have kids with. I'm goddamn lonely!

Instead all she says is: "Oh, nothing. I'm just tired, that's all."

"Well, it's no wonder; you've been getting so little sleep lately. And I'll bet you're not eating enough either, hmm?"

"I don't even know what we're doing here," Clara grumbles quietly to herself.

Her mother tries to get a smile out of her: "Oh, honey. Having doubts is part of the process. But you're well on your way to turning your hobby into a career. And that's a wonderful thing! Lots of people would envy you for this opportunity."

"I know. I'm not trying to sound ungrateful. But what if I waste all of Grandma's money?" Clara can't stand up anymore. Her legs give out. She slides slowly down the wall and ends up crouching down on the floor of the long, narrow hallway in her apartment. In this position she feels even smaller than usual. She can't help thinking of the hopeful smiles on Lisbeth's and Willy's faces when the two of them proudly announced that they would like to use the inheritance from Lisbeth's aunt to support her in her career as a painter.

"But they're happy to give you the money! And it's not as though they'd been counting on receiving an inheritance. Definitely not such a large one. But you can do something really meaningful with it!"

"Ugh, and what if they wanted to travel around the world? Would that be any less meaningful?"

Her mother kneels down close to her and looks at her lovingly.

"But honey, what would you do if you were in their place? Don't you think they would give anything they could to see you happy again?"

Suddenly Clara feels even smaller. What she really wants more than anything is for someone to put her arms around her and just let her go to sleep. For her mother to never leave her again. Clara is all mixed up. All the paintings around her are full of emotion—and yet they represent the same feelings over and over again.

"Why did you always dump me with them?" The words suddenly burst out of her. She can't look her mother in the eye and buries her face in her hands.

"Why did I what? I . . . dumped you?" Karin asks so softly that Clara can barely hear her. "I thought you always liked being with your grandparents?"

Clara lifts her head and looks her mother right in the eye. The look on her face is glowering. "Of course I did. That's because they were there for me when I needed them."

For a few moments there is only silence.

"And I wasn't there for you?" Clara's mother asks, stunned. She sits down next to Clara on the floor.

Clara feels a lump in her throat. Tears well up inside her, but she tries to choke them back as best she can.

Karin asks a second time: "What's going on in that head of yours? Talk to me!"

"Ugh, you probably don't even care."

"What? . . . What did I do to you? Did I say something wrong?"

"You didn't say anything! That's the problem . . ." Clara gives her mother a furious look.

"Didn't say anything about what, for heaven's sake?"

"Like about why you just took off after Dad died!"

Karin has to let this accusation sink in before she can respond. She stands back up, looks down at Clara, and says seriously: "So you think I went off and had a nice vacation while you grieved alone with Lisbeth and Willy?"

Clara looks meekly at the floor. A tear rolls down her cheek; she can't help it. She shrugs her shoulders.

"But you know I needed distance from all of it. I always thought being with the two of them was the best place for you to be."

"I was still alone."

"And I was at the end of my rope. How was I supposed to be there for you when I was lost myself?"

"Oh, don't give me that. You were happy that Dad was finally out of the way!"

"Clara!" Karin shouts. Clara has never heard her shout like that before.

Now Clara stands up as well. She draws herself up, looks right at her mother and says: "Other than at the funeral I never once saw you crying!" The moment she says this, Clara regrets her harsh words. She bites her lip.

The corners of Karin's mouth start to tremble. She stares at Clara in disbelief and places a hand on her arm.

"Clara. Please believe me, when I think of your dad and how much he suffered, it still feels like the wind's been knocked out of me. It's true I was relieved when he was finally released from the pain he was in. But to this day I still love him—just as much as I love you!" There's a tremor in her voice now. After a short while she continues: "How many times do you think I sat crying in silence, long after you'd gone to bed?"

Clara lets out a breath—she hadn't exhaled all the time Clara was talking—and now asks: "But why did you never say anything?"

"I always tried to spare you from having to see too much of all of that. It went back to when your dad urged me not to tell you anything about his illness for as long as I could. We wanted you to have as carefree a life as possible!"

"But maybe that just made it even worse."

"Oh, honey, come here," her mother whispers and puts her arms around Clara. Her embrace is gentle and yet firm enough that for a moment Clara feels like a pitiful little kid.

Suddenly Clara can't find the words for everything else she still wants to say to her mother. But for the first time in her life she feels like her mother understands her—and without any uselessly long explanations.

Karin strokes her hair. She speaks again in a soft voice: "I know that I didn't do everything right back then. But like any mother I only ever wanted what was best for my child! You would try to shield your daughter as much as you could, too."

"But I'll probably never have kids!" Clara says feebly, her face still buried in her mother's shoulder.

"Of course you will, if that's what you want. You'll find a new person to love. Someone different, but without a doubt someone who will give you a child. And all that I would wish for is that your child be just as enchanting a person as you are. And that's exactly why Lisbeth and Willy are giving you the money—because it's in good hands with you and they love you more than anything."

Clara can't help it anymore now. She can't get out another word. She's sobbing so hard that she can hardly breathe.

Before she found the courage to say something to her mother about how worried she was that she would never have children, Clara hadn't really been aware of how much of a concern this clearly was for her. She'd always thought that Ben's asking her to marry him automatically meant yes to having a child. Because he wanted children, too; Clara knew he did.

On just their second date at Cheers Clara had been impressed by the casual way Ben had of getting right to the heart of whatever matter he was speaking about. He had come home with her, kissed her passionately as soon as they got through the door, and then asked her to give him the full tour of her apartment— including the bedroom. He had stopped in front of a photo of Clara as a child.

"When I'm grown up, I'd like to have a couple of cute little rug rats myself. How about you?"

Clara has to smile at the memory of him saying this. But it comes with a bitter aftertaste. How naive they'd been! Not once had they discussed the subject in a mature, detailed way.

Nevertheless, in all the years she was with Ben she had never really doubted that she would have children. She had even felt sorry for people like Katja who made a conscious decision not to have kids. Even if Clara can no longer bear to be around some of her old friends these days because their world revolves entirely around their children, she had always told herself that she would do it all differently. She'd always wanted to try to have a career and not become one of these mothers who isn't interested in anything anymore besides diapers and baby clothes. And she was so happy to have found in Ben a partner who seemed to feel the same way she did.

But now that she's read the farewell letter her suspicion has turned to certainty: Children would have meant responsibility, and Ben probably felt a lot of pressure whenever she raised the subject. Or had he just possessed far more foresight than she did? Had he known, or sensed, that they were both still far too deeply stuck in their own childhoods? Would they have been at all capable of instilling in their child the basic sense of trust that all children need?

Clara feels a lump in her throat. After everything that has happened in the past few months, the desire for a child has faded so far into the background that for the first time in her life she's not sure anymore if she really would like to be a mother someday. She feels like she's at a crossroads with too many turnings and not a single one of them is marked.

But she's happy that she has her family. Her mother and her grandparents. And in this moment Clara is filled with a massive feeling of gratitude. She hugs her mother even tighter. Finally she can let her mother see her feeling small or weak. And she's also very thankful to have received such a generous gift from Lisbeth and Willy. She'll be able to afford the rent for her own studio for some time, even if self-employment doesn't work out quite as she'd dreamed it would.

Clara senses a fresh surge of energy flowing through her body. She nods at her mother; things are okay now between them. First thing tomorrow she's going to load up the car and take her best paintings to Beppo at the restaurant.

Maybe I should invite my family and friends out for dinner at Castello, thinks Clara. *This weekend, for example, I could celebrate the kickoff of my new era of professional freedom and thank those dear to me for all their wonderful support. Actually next Saturday is just about ideal.* Clara is warming to the idea even more—because Saturday is her birthday.

Up until now the day has been a source of dread more than anything else. It's her first birthday without Ben, and after the great celebration last year, she wasn't sure what she should do this year. But now she has a reason to actually look forward to it!

Clara decides to give Ben the good news this very night.

sven

Sven looks thoughtfully out the window of his office at the many cranes working without cease on the harbor. Again his thoughts are on Clara and yesterday evening in Lüneburg.

He walked around the Old City for more than three hours. The longer he walked the streets, the more beautiful, but also eerie, the atmosphere that was given off by all these small, eccentric buildings seemed to him. It seemed fitting that he was on the lookout for a woman he barely knew anything about—not what she looked like, not even if she really existed at all. Sure, he knew there was a Clara in Lüneburg whose heart was broken and whom he found fascinating, despite the fact or maybe even because of it. But he has no idea if the image he's formed of an imaginary Clara comes even close to resembling the real person.

Sven would so like to know how she's going to manage to take control of her circumstances. Even if he knows as good as nothing about her relationship with this mysterious Ben, he still suspects that in her texts, and in her paintings for sure, Clara is expressing what she feels.

The few times he talked to people on the street to ask about a painter he was looking for named Clara, he remained very guarded. It seemed strange to him, as if he were afraid of getting even one step closer to the real Clara.

But even after three hours he hadn't really gotten any closer to finding her. No trace of a young, talented painter named Clara. Finally Sven went to a bar and found a table.

There were indeed a great many similar-looking establishments lined up one after the other in the narrow streets. Sven thought this place called Cheers looked particularly inviting somehow. He ordered a steak and a pilsner and sat reading the regional paper with interest. He thought maybe chance would send him a clue.

But chance waited until about an hour and a half later, when he was headed back home, driving out of the city and toward the highway, frustrated. He came to a stop at a big intersection where he was supposed to turn left. He was just considering whether he should maybe take a different route when he heard his phone go off—he'd gotten a text.

> Thank you again for leading me to Castello. I'm going to make the best of my birthday—just like you did last year, I promise! L.

Sven almost hollered for joy. His trip to Lüneburg hadn't been for nothing! He would go find this Castello place right away.

At the same moment the light turned green. Grinning, he told himself that it was a sign and drove off. At the next gas station he made a quick stop and asked for directions to the restaurant.

And sure enough, after another thirty minutes of twists and turns he saw a sign on the right side of the road. Above a wooden gate were the words "Castello—Fine Italian Wine and Cuisine." The lights weren't on, so Sven slowed down, which immediately earned him a barrage of honks from the car behind him. Normally Sven would have flown off the handle and cursed the driver out. But he was so happy to have made this discovery that he let the guy pass without complaint and reverently followed the very long driveway that led to Castello.

With heart pounding he drove right up to the parking lot and immediately saw that the restaurant was closed. But the feeling that he was in the right place was so captivating that he wasn't willing to let this dampen his spirits.

He turned off the engine and walked up to the front door to look for the restaurant's hours. Closed Mondays. *Typical*, thought Sven.

On the wall to the left of the front door was a glass case in which part of the menu could be seen. Only a feeble bit of light from the street reached the little box, and Sven had a hard time reading the menu inside. But not only did he see there was a Pizza Diavola on the menu, he also found the owners' names: Giuseppe and Marina Ventorino. Giuseppe could well be Beppo. Sven silently rejoiced.

He tried to get a look through the small windows. As far as he could tell there were indeed a few paintings on the walls inside the restaurant, but they weren't moon paintings. Still, now he knew where he could look for Clara next.

Calm and contented, he started heading back to Hamburg. A big smile came to his face when, as he was searching through different radio stations, he suddenly heard the song "Wish You

Were Here" by Pink Floyd. He sang along at the top of his lungs—and in the best of moods.

* * *

"Are you done yet?"

This is now the fourth time Hilke has asked him this annoying question. Finally he wrenches his gaze from the cranes in the harbor and turns to his colleague, who is nervously rummaging in her purse—she can't find her car keys.

"Admit it," she whines, "you hid my keys so that you can go to Lüneburg without me. Right?"

Sven gives his colleague an admonitory look and frowns. Actually he still has to finish writing an important email, but all day long he's had a hard time concentrating. Though he's trying to hide his nervousness, it feels like anyone could tell how worked up he is from a distance of thirty feet.

In just a moment he and his colleague are going to drive to Lüneburg and have dinner at Castello. Sven hopes to use the opportunity to learn more about Clara from the proprietor. On the phone this afternoon Giuseppe Ventorino didn't seem at all surprised that a journalist would be interested in paintings that hadn't even gone on view yet. He was more than happy to provide information, saying that the young artist had kindly agreed to make her thoroughly well-executed work available for public viewing, starting this weekend. He grew so effusive as he spoke about the *bella ragazza* and her paintings that Sven couldn't help thinking that the chatty chef didn't just have an eye out for nice ways to decorate his bare walls; he must also have a tidy commission coming to him if the paintings sold well.

"There, found 'em. Let's go!" Hilke says in a tone of voice that makes her sound like an army drill sergeant.

"You're driving me nuts! Can I please finish this email to the finance minister?" Sven snarls back in the same tone. But Hilke doesn't seem one bit fazed.

Just twenty minutes later, they're turning off the A1 and merging onto the A250, Lüneburg bound. Sven couldn't be happier that Hilke has been on the phone the whole time. She's attempting to mollify her mother-in-law after she and her son butted heads at dinner last night. What Sven is less pleased about is the fact that Hilke is doing this without a hands-free device and while driving at what feels like a hundred miles per hour.

Here the opportunity has finally presented itself for him to find out more about the mysterious Clara, and just before accomplishing his aim, he's probably going to die a horrible death—or at least he will if Hilke keeps driving like a maniac. He gestures at her, trying to get her to slow down a bit. But she seems to be in even more of a hurry to get there than he is.

Hilke is too curious for her own good, Sven thinks. Naturally she also got to experience the phone call with Beppo in real time. But Sven has to admit that it's a big help to have her come along with him this evening. Even if he might not get answers to all of his questions, he'll at least be one step closer to finding Clara.

And if nothing else, thanks to Beppo he now knows that Clara's last name is Sommerfeld. And if the guy from the Lüneburg city hall could have just made an exception instead of getting so pissy about it, Sven would also know her address or at least her date of birth by now. Unfortunately the internet didn't provide any useful information either, to say nothing of a photo.

So Clara is still faceless. What Sven would like to do now is to swap ideas with Hilke, to speculate on whether she might be a blonde or a brunette, thin or curvy, attractive or plain.

But he figures he'd better hold off. Hilke is off the phone now at least, but every time a car pulls out in front of them Sven is stepping on an imaginary brake pedal in the passenger seat and getting ever more tense. Not that Hilke lets this bother her; she remains intent on getting her Opel from one Hanseatic city to another in record time.

"Are you really hungry, is that why you're in such a hurry?" Sven asks carefully.

"Haha! I'm so worked up I couldn't eat a single bite right now," Hilke replies.

"Well, we're going to have to eat something. We can't just walk in there like a couple of TV detectives, ask a few uncomfortable questions, and then leave," he says.

"So I think it's the next exit" is Hilke's only reply.

Sven is starting to feel a bit queasy. There's a lump in his throat. *What if by chance Clara happens to be there?* he asks himself. A situation like that would really be more than he could handle, not least because he's got Hilke with him, who keeps constantly teasing him and telling him he's like a teenager who's about to say "I love you" for the first time.

When they finally turn into the restaurant's driveway and Sven sees the illuminated sign, his heart gives a little leap. All the embarrassment that he feels with Hilke around always staring at him with her X-ray eyes gives way to extreme excitement.

They park in front of the building, and the sight of the entrance already seems strangely familiar to Sven.

Gallantly he holds the door open for Hilke, follows her into the restaurant, and walks right up to a short, fat man who looks just as Sven had imagined Beppo would look on the telephone.

"Good evening. I have a reservation."

"*Un momento*, please!" says the man and nods at an attractive waitress who with her light blond hair looks anything but Italian.

"Hello, good evening," she says politely. "You reserved a table?"

"Yes, under the name Lehmann."

She looks at a little book, crosses out an entry, and says: "Come with me; it's just through here. Or would you rather sit outside on the terrace?"

"No!" Hilke and Sven say at the same time and both give each other an annoyed look.

From the front room they now proceed into a stylishly decorated, cozy dining room with ten or so tables, about half of which are occupied. On the other side of the hallway voices and laughter can be heard; it sounds like a larger party. *There must be several more rooms in addition to this one*, thinks Sven, *plus the seats outside.*

Somewhat awkwardly, he lets the waitress take his jacket after she's taken Hilke's, and he sits down in the chair opposite his colleague. As the friendly waitress lights candles and asks if she might offer them an aperitif, he looks around, searching. No sign of Clara's paintings anywhere. But unlike last night the walls are all bare. There are only a few small framed mirrors hanging on one side of the room with tall white candles burning on pretty metal holders to the left and right of them. And on the opposite wall there are what is clearly a very old clock and two framed Monet prints hanging between the front windows.

Hilke seems to catch on to Sven's disappointment. She turns to the waitress, who is just handing each of them a menu, and asks baldly: "Tell me, I've heard that there are supposed to be paintings by a young artist on view here soon."

The woman smiles and answers: "Yes, Clara Sommerfeld. They're really beautiful pieces. The exhibit isn't officially open yet, but a few paintings are already up in our private dining room."

"Ah, thanks. Could we maybe take a look at them?" Clara asks with a stunningly friendly smile. And Sven is worried that she might just jump up to go see them right now.

"Mmm, I imagine so. At the moment though we've got a private party in there. Would you mind waiting a bit?"

"Sure—if that's not going to be too much torture for you!" Hilke whispers smugly to Sven and flashes a gleefully malicious grin.

Sven sneaks a look at the menu.

The next grin adorns Hilke's face when, a short while later, she orders a wine spritzer, carpaccio, and for her main course a Pizza Diavola. Sven feels a bit overwhelmed and hastily orders the mixed antipasti plate, filet of beef with gorgonzola, a pilsner, and a whiskey.

Hilke looks at him with surprise. Although Sven feels the need to explain the whiskey, he declines to—it would only make this whole scene even more unpleasant. He's feverishly thinking about how he might steer the conversation back to work or some other innocuous subject when Hilke jumps up, flashes another grin, and says, "I'm off to the ladies'!"

Sven shakes his head. He can scarcely believe that he's putting himself through this. He looks around the restaurant again, and in spite of himself, little by little, something like a pleasant mood seems to take hold deep inside him. *Clara must have good taste*, he thinks, *if this is her favorite spot*. The thought that she was here a short time ago to hang up her paintings even brings a dreamy little smile to his lips. Suddenly he feels like a little boy just before Christmas morning, so excited about his gifts that he can hardly bear it.

After what feels like forever, Hilke comes back to the table.

"Amazing! So cool. I knew it. The woman's got talent!"

"You didn't actually go in there!" Sven cries angrily and feels like crawling under his chair.

"Now don't be so uptight. Nobody noticed."

"And? Are the paintings really okay?" Sven asks, unable to hide his curiosity.

"Oh yeah. The colors alone! Totally balanced. I'd hang a painting like that in my apartment in a second. Or in the office, so I can actually look at something nice for a change," Hilke replies and blows Sven a kiss just to rub it in.

Before Sven can respond, the waitress comes back to the table with their drinks, plus some bread and butter.

"To a successful evening!" Hilke says smugly. She raises her wine spritzer to clink glasses with Sven and then adds a threat: "God help you if you don't make anything of it!"

. . .

After the appetizer Sven excuses himself and goes to the bathroom, but even though Hilke has kept urging him nonstop to go take a peek in the next room already, he stands in the hallway for a long time, indecisive. Only when Beppo comes hurrying past does he awake from his lethargy.

"Excuse me. Do you know the artist whose work is on display in the next room personally?"

"*Sì, sì, signore!* Clara Sommerfeld, a young and very promising talent. We've even had reporters calling to ask about her!" Beppo says, his chest swelling with pride. He could be talking about his own daughter.

Sven clears his throat and hesitates to let Beppo know it was he who called. "Um, yes. I'm also a journalist and I'd like to meet the young lady sometime."

The Italian looks at him in surprise, eyes him for a second, and then says with a big grin, "Of course I can't just give you her number. But you could meet her here if you like. On Saturday, I will have the honor of spoiling her with my humble cuisine." Beppo keeps grinning his friendly grin and looks at his guest expectantly.

Sven doesn't really know how to respond; his thoughts are already on this weekend.

Beppo goes on in his friendly way. "Maybe it's best you leave me your number. Then I'll be glad to pass it on to Signorina Sommerfeld."

"Sounds good," Sven quickly replies. He reaches in his back pocket for his wallet and pulls out a business card. He hands it to Beppo and, hoping to avoid any doubt, adds, "I'm a business journalist and right now I'm working on an article about young artists. It would be nice if you could let Miss Sommerfeld know that there's a bit of a rush."

When Sven comes back to the table, Hilke is looking at him with eyes wide, waiting to hear an explanation. Clearly from where she was sitting she was perfectly placed to observe his conversation with Beppo.

"Well, what do you have to say for yourself?"

"About what?" Sven grins.

"I'm gonna snap that neck of yours like a twig!" Hilke threatens. "Don't you think the paintings are out of this world?"

"I never went in there. But I did see to it that our nice rotund Italian friend passes along my card." He leans back, satisfied, while Hilke stares at him in exasperation.

"And now you're just going to do what, sit on your hands and wait?"

"No, I'm going to drink beer and wait." Sven reaches for his pilsner, raises his glass, and toasts his colleague without a word.

Hilke rolls her eyes, glances quickly to her left and right, and then hisses in a tone that brooks no further discussion: "I just have one thing to tell you. I'm not leaving here until you've gone and looked at those great paintings!"

But only after they've eaten does Sven hazard another attempt. The private dining room has long since emptied out and all the lights have been turned off. But there's still so much light shining into the room from the bar area that he ventures a few steps inside. Right away he's surprised at both the size of the paintings and how many of them there are. He guesses there must be more than twenty of them.

Stepping gingerly, he walks up to the first painting on the wall to his left. Even in the half-darkened room the full, deep red that extends over the entire surface of the painting seems to really shine. The silvery, shimmering moon immediately catches his eye, standing out against the background, strangely luminescent, and radiating something mysterious and yet very peaceful. A few inches below the canvas is a little label: "Blood Moon, 220 €."

Sven's gaze drifts down to the bottom right edge of the painting, where a white signature is visible. He takes another step closer, now he can read it. It says only "Clara S." but the style that shows in the lettering brings a smile to Sven's lips.

clara

ypical, thinks Clara as her birthday guests take their seats around the large table. *Everyone's on time, just not Katja.* Amused, Clara wonders if her friend's lateness could have anything to do with the two big surprises she mentioned.

Clara hasn't felt this good, this all-around content, for a long time. She looks around the room with a smile and is thankful to have all the people she loves with her. Her mother and her partner Reinhard, Lisbeth and Willy, Bea, and Dorothea—even Ben's mother is here; Dorothea had managed to convince her to accept Clara's invitation, and Clara is truly glad to finally be seeing the two of them on a joyous occasion again. Today she'll be showing her best paintings, full of joy and pride, and even Ben seems to be present somehow.

Clara is so excited that she doesn't feel at all hungry. Not that this would stop Beppo, who has already started bringing out various delicacies on giant white porcelain platters. And right at this moment, almost as if she could sense that the food was being served, Katja comes tiptoeing around the corner. But rather than walking up and joining the large group at the table right away, she waves Clara over to her.

"Hey, babe, let me hug you. I wish you all the happiness in the world. You've really earned it!" Katja singsongs in her ear, hugging her so tight that Clara doesn't catch every word. She's still got a lump in her throat all the same, but she fights back the tears.

"Thanks! But now tell me, where are the surprises?" Clara draws herself up in front of her friend, eyebrows raised and arms crossed over her chest. Given all the crazy ideas that Katja has already come up with, she fears the worst. But there's such a radiant gleam in her friend's eyes that Clara can tell she must have something really wonderful up her sleeve.

"They're both just around the corner here." Katja turns around and calls out, "Andy? You can come out now!"

Mouth agape and eyes goggling, Clara stares at the incredibly attractive man who now walks in holding a large, flat box wrapped in brown paper in his left hand. He offers his right hand to Clara with a winning and slightly embarrassed smile.

"Happy birthday! I'm Andreas. Actually we kind of know each other already from that speed-dating event. Katja just dragged me here with her, so I'm totally innocent in all this and hope it's all right with you that I'm here?"

Clara gives Katja a meaningful look and replies, "Of course it's all right. I have no idea how we're ever going to manage all this food. Have a seat, you two!"

"In a second, but I have something else to say first," Katja proclaims ceremoniously and looks around the room, inviting the group's attention. She grabs a glass of prosecco off the tray that the quick-thinking waitress has just brought over. Then she clears her throat.

"My dearest friend! All of us here know that this day can't be easy for you. Which makes it all the more important for you to know how happy we all are to see you smiling again. What I couldn't manage to do in countless attempts to cheer you up, you manage to do all by yourself with these paintings of yours! You sit down, grab your brushes, start mixing paints and other materials like a madwoman, and out comes this!" Katja gestures toward the canvasses, whose full colors create a warm atmosphere. The gentle light of the countless white candles in the room enhances the mood even further.

Karin starts to applaud, and all the others immediately follow her example and join in. Then Katja continues.

"In any case, your painting puts this wonderful smile on your lips, and you should be incredibly proud of your talent. But in order to ensure that all this doesn't just continue to be a nice way to pass the time and that you start making some real dough from this hobby of yours, I, in consultation with your grandmother, have found a studio for you in the Old City. You can go see it first thing Monday morning. And for a little insurance, just to make sure you don't back out, I've got a nice little present here for you."

She signals to Andy and he hands Clara the flat package. Clara feels like she's in a movie that's playing in slow motion. Now Beppo, his wife, and the server have also appeared in the wide doorway and are watching with curiosity. Just like the others, they're anxious to see Clara rip open the thick paper.

A light gray acrylic sign comes into view, with large, silvery-blue cursive lettering that reads: "Art and Praxis." Just like they'd come up with on one of their last brainstorming nights.

Clara can't believe it—she's speechless. She hugs Katja and Andy in quick succession. The others cheer and clap their hands.

If she could, Clara would just stop time to preserve this special moment. Then maybe she would be able to take in all the wonderful things that are happening all at once: her first exhibition, which could well lead to many more in galleries and cultural institutions, and now her very own studio in Lüneburg's Old City. She trusts Katja's expertise. What's more, she has the necessary start-up capital and already has a fabulous sign. And the first buyer has already approached Beppo, a person who is prepared to pay an unbelievable 270 euros for a painting by her. Plus apparently a reporter was asking about her. But above all it's the many generous people around her who have helped turn this day that she had so dreaded into something wonderful.

Clara can really feel the prosecco going to her head. Cheerfully she smiles, half in a daze, and clinks glasses with every single one of her guests before finally digging into the delicious food.

sven

Curious, Sven looks down from his roof terrace at the flocks of people here for the neighborhood street festival and the many cars that crawl along at a snail's pace, trying to squeeze through the narrow streets around the pedestrian zone. Whenever he sees a driver looking in vain for a parking space, he silently congratulates himself—so far he's gotten along quite well in his life without a car.

But last night he deeply regretted not having one at his disposal. Otherwise he would definitely have mustered the courage to drive back down to Lüneburg. True, over the course of the last week Hilke had offered to let him use her car about twenty times. But he didn't want to take advantage of either her readiness to help or her curiosity and find himself driving the Opel—or even worse, the Opel *and* Hilke—back to Castello. The last thing he wants to do is to just waylay Clara on her birthday or to try to force a meeting in some other contrived way.

Not really knowing what to do with himself last night, he called his father. And he's very happy that he did, because the two of them had a really relaxed evening together.

Sven had to grin when his old dad offered to take him out to an

Italian restaurant of all places. Contrary to his expectations it turned out to be a totally nice evening. They even talked a little about Sven's mother—what would have been her seventieth birthday was coming up soon.

But this Sunday is going to need a little work if there's to be any hope of salvaging it, thinks Sven. Not even the intense workout this morning was enough to settle him down.

Like an insufferable teenager he keeps losing himself in fantasies of what it might be like when Clara finally called. It strikes him as almost ironic, as though fate were continuing to play its little games with him, that he's long had the mysterious Lilime's phone number but nevertheless can't contact her, because officially she only knows his work number and email address.

Still, Sven had gone to the trouble of setting up call forwarding so that he would receive any calls to his work phone on his cell. And he had also linked his personal email account to his work account so that all his work emails, which he normally wouldn't even glance at in his free time, would reach him at home.

But so far there was no word from Clara. Sven is ardently hoping that this Beppo character didn't forget to pass on his business card. He figures it would have been yesterday at the latest, when she was at the restaurant, that Beppo would have let her know. And if she's actually interested in having a conversation, then really she should be getting in touch first thing next week.

But what if she's not at all interested?

"Oh, man!" Sven pounds the steel railing with the flat of his hand and shakes his head. He just can't believe that his thoughts are back on Clara again. He has to get his mind off her.

Just when he's decided to ask David if he feels like grabbing a beer at one of the stands down on the street, his phone dings.

It's a text from Clara! *Now of all times*, thinks Sven. After such a long break, she apparently feels the urge to talk.

> I'm now completely determined to strike out on my own and be an artist. You made it possible! Thank you for the wonderful birthday present. Love, L.

Right away Sven is in a better mood. Clara seems significantly more carefree than she did just a short while ago. He'd really like to tell someone about it.

David doesn't answer, unfortunately, so he sets himself up with a beer on the terrace and thinks about other ways he might be able to get in touch with Clara.

No matter what, tomorrow morning at the Monday editorial meeting he's going to propose the "young freelancers" topic to his boss again. After all, he'd already done some research on the market for freelancers a short while ago. All he's missing is the most up-to-date numbers and two or three potential interview subjects. What with the recession, though, he's confident he can convince Breiding to give the go-ahead for an article on such a highly relevant topic.

· · ·

When he gets back to his desk the next morning after three tedious hours stuck in the editorial meeting, Sven is pleased: Sure enough, his proposal met with interest. Hilke, however, meets his optimism with skepticism. "Well?" she asks him. "Anything of note happen this weekend? Any word from the Lüneburg art scene?"

Sven rolls his eyes with annoyance and just lets out a loud sigh.

"Just be happy you've got somebody thoughtful like me to concern herself with your well-being," Hilke responds angrily.

"Well, thank you very much," Sven replies sarcastically. He sits down in his chair and tries to change the subject. He quickly pushes to the back of his mind the mild disappointment he feels that there's been no word from Clara yet. No way does he want to encourage Hilke's laughable interpretation of his supposedly more positive recent attitude by giving her cause to believe there's a whiff of romance behind it.

He moves his mouse and the screensaver gives way to the desktop. His email client is indicating that he has seventeen new messages. He clicks to open it and a small thrill suddenly courses through his body—in the middle of the unread emails he finds one with the subject line "Responding to Your Inquiry" from sender "c.sommerfeld@artandpraxis.de."

While Hilke comments on how the editorial meeting went, Sven tries to casually open the email and not let anything show.

"Yeah, yeah, we've got the topics for the next few months. It'll come together one way or another," Sven mutters vaguely, as if he were about to fall asleep—while on the inside he's electrified. Filled with excitement, he reads Clara's email.

From: c.sommerfeld@artandpraxis.de

Subject: Responding to Your Inquiry

Dear Mr. Lehmann,

Mr. Ventorino from the Lüneburg restaurant Castello gave me your card and passed along your request that I contact you.

I'd be happy to speak to you in connection with the article you're researching. You can contact me any time at the number below.

Yours sincerely,
Clara Sommerfeld

Sven reads these lines at least three times in quick succession and then just stares at his computer screen, clearly dumbstruck. Seeing him, Hilke asks, "Everything all right? You've got this weird look on your face."

"Oh, yeah, yeah. I'm just reading. But we men are no good at multitasking, you know that." He flashes her a brief smile and then turns his full attention back to his inbox. He can't possibly call Clara right now. Hilke would be breathing down his neck trying to make sure she caught every word. Sven follows his impulse and clicks Reply instead.

He himself doesn't really understand it, but in a strange way this email simply overwhelms him, even though it's so much more dry and businesslike than everything else she's ever written. Maybe it's the fact that he now knows for certain that he's actually going to meet this woman face-to-face one day. *And this day isn't at all far off either,* he thinks. *After all, I've got to have a four-thousand-word article written in just two weeks.*

Sven takes his first crack at a reply:

From: Sven Lehmann

Subject: RE: Responding to Your Inquiry

Hello Ms. Sommerfeld—

He tries again.

Dear Ms. Sommerfeld,

Thank you for your quick reply.

At the moment I'm working on an article for the magazine on
young freelancers—

Sven deletes "young" and can't help grinning all of a sudden.

"What are you smiling about?" Nothing escapes Hilke; she
seems to be watching his every move.

"Oh, just some raunchy joke email from a buddy of mine. You'd
just get all worked up about it if I showed you."

"Men!" Hilke groans and disappears behind her computer
screen.

Then Sven continues:

I'd like to interview you about your transition into self-employment,
and if you're willing, I'd also like to include a short profile of you in
my article as a way of providing our readers with an example of
someone working in your field.

Though I realize it's short notice, I'd be grateful if you could come
to our offices for an interview in the next few days . . .

Sven ditches the last line—immediately upon writing it he
imagined the awkward situation that would arise if Hilke were
around when Clara showed up.

I'm happy to come to Lüneburg if you can find the time and know
of a suitable place to meet.

Thanks very much and warm regards . . .

He replaces "warm regards" with "best regards," types his name at the bottom, and hits Send. He sneaks a look over at Hilke, who at that moment stands up to go get some coffee. Immediately she asks, "What is it?"

Sven shrugs his shoulders and says airily, "Nothing. Why do you ask?"

clara

f this week gets any more exciting I won't make it to my next birthday, thinks Clara as she looks in the mirror and puts mascara on. On Monday, she went and saw the wonderful, marvelous, yes, simply perfect studio. On Tuesday, she signed the lease and got a call from Beppo with the good news that two more paintings had been sold. Yesterday, she finished putting together a brochure with the help of Sandra, the agency's copywriter. And today, she was meeting with this journalist. Clara has no idea what to expect, and it shows in how nervous she is.

But hey, the guy came to her. He wants something from her and not the other way around. She'll just have to answer a few questions, that's all.

So calm down and try to look forward to a nice evening, she admonishes herself. If nothing else, Mr. Lehmann is coming down from Hamburg specially for this interview, so it would be very impolite to cancel now at the last minute. Katja would give her a kick in the ass, if not something worse, if Clara let this opportunity for free PR slip away just like that. Clara finds a small amount of reassurance in the fact that he agreed to meet at

Cheers. Ben is especially close to her there. He'll protect her from anything upsetting.

· · ·

But by the time Clara is headed to Cheers on her bike about thirty minutes later, she's really freaking out. What if she can't come up with a single substantial or interesting answer to any of his questions? She herself doesn't have a clue what she's doing. Like all the legal stuff that she still has to find time to sit down and study. And the financial stuff, too. According to his business card, this Lehmann guy is a reporter for the business section; he'll be an absolute expert and will immediately realize that he'd picked the wrong person.

Anxiously Clara gets off her bike, locks it up on a rack, and realizes angrily that it's right in front of the window. Mr. Lehmann has probably been here for a while already and can see her from inside. But when she walks in, there's not a single customer in the place. Clara figures Mr. Lehmann to be in his midfifties, a bit overweight, more on the unattractive side, but polite and impeccably dressed. That's what she imagines a business reporter at an important magazine would look like, anyway.

She walks to an empty table in the back right corner of the bar, sits down where she can keep an eye on the door, and orders a latte macchiato.

I'm early. I've got time to prepare a few clever lines before he gets here, the kind that'll make me sound super-casual and confident, like a real tough-as-nails businesswoman, thinks Clara. But inside she feels completely different, more like a little schoolgirl about to take an exam that will decide whether she advances to the next grade or gets held back a year.

She takes out her phone in case Mr. Lehmann tries to call. *He ought to be here any moment,* she thinks. She reaches into her purse to look at his business card again. She studies it and tries to keep herself calm.

But Clara keeps anxiously looking at the door. Just like that day years ago when she was keeping an eye out for Katja, who, as always, was late. Ben was sitting at the table next to her and asked, half cheeky, half polite, if she'd been stood up. Since he had also been waiting for a friend who never showed up, eventually he just slid his chair over and joined her. The night turned out to be surprisingly fun. Ben didn't waste any time: "You're not from Lüneburg, are you? No way, you can't be—I'm sure I would have noticed such a pretty face before!"

Right as Clara feels her eyes filling with tears at the memory of how she and Ben first met, her phone rings.

sven

S uch bullshit!" Sven curses to himself. This damn train picks today of all days to actually be on time for once!

He got to the platform just in time to see the train pulling away. For a second he considered whether he should come clean to Hilke about his date and ask her to borrow her car again. But she'd no doubt be pissed that he kept quiet about it for days, even lied a little to cover it up. Plus if he waited and took the next train to Lüneburg he'd still probably make it there faster than if he were to take the subway from Altona out to Hilke's place in Winterhude and then have to deal with rush-hour traffic on the highway. *But the next train won't get me to Lüneburg on time, either,* thinks Sven—and he just can't believe that after searching forever for a pay phone, the one he finally manages to find is out of order.

And because he can't very well use Ben's phone—that is, his phone with Ben's number—to call Clara and apologize for being late, he's starting to get the feeling that fate is trying to screw him over. Maybe it's punishment for all the lies he's told. But really, thus far he hasn't misled Clara at all. In a situation like this, though, he has to tread lightly. He can't possibly go barreling in by calling Clara up and confusing her completely.

"Excuse me!" Sven approaches an elderly woman.

"Yes?" she politely replies.

"Do you happen to have a cell phone I could use?" he asks.

"Sorry, I don't—but that young man over there is bound to have one," she says and gestures toward a teenager who, with a baseball cap pulled low over his forehead and earbuds plugged into his MP3 player, has completely closed himself off to the outside world.

"Thanks," says Sven and turns to the kid, who he guesses must be about fifteen.

"Excuse me!" Sven speaks extra loudly.

"Why are you yelling?"

"Sorry, I thought . . ." Sven points to his ears, miming to indicate the earbuds.

The kid gives Sven a surly look, waiting for him to get to the point.

"Uh, could you maybe lend me your cell phone? I have to make an urgent call."

"What's in it for me?"

"Well, you'll be helping out your fellow man in his time of need."

"Huh?"

"All right fine." Sven rummages in his wallet for a two-euro coin and puts it in the kid's hand.

The kid looks at the coin and scowls. Then he sticks his hand out again and puts on a poker face.

Sven's patience is already worn thin, but he's got no other choice.

"This is extortion!" he grouses. He takes out a five-euro bill and hands it over, though not before snatching back the two-euro coin.

Finally the kid hands over his phone. "Just don't take too long!" Sven frowns and looks through his iPhone for Clara's number.

"But you've already got a phone!" the kid shouts indignantly. "A really sweet phone!" In one quick motion he snatches his own phone back out of Sven's hand and tries to run off.

"Stop!" Sven shouts, apparently with such authority that the kid actually does stop. He looks a bit intimidated now. "I can't use mine right now, got it?"

"Technology too much for you, huh?" The kid grins, shakes his head, and sticks his hand out again.

"You're a no-good, scheming little brat!" Sven snarls and again hands the kid the two-euro piece in exchange for his cell phone.

Nervously he types the number into the display. It rings.

He hears Clara's clear, warm voice whisper "Yes?" on the other end of the line, and it takes what seems like an hour before he's finally able to tamp down his anger and hide his agitation.

"Ms. Sommerfeld? Sven Lehmann here. I'm sorry, but I didn't manage to catch my train." His surroundings there at the Altona train station are fairly loud, but Sven does his best to maintain a mild tone of voice.

"Come again? I can't hear you very well. You'll have to speak a little louder!"

"This is Sven Lehmann. I missed my train and won't be able to get out there to meet you for another forty-five minutes."

"Oh" is all Clara says.

"I'm sorry. Would you be able to wait, or should we figure out another time?"

Clara seems to hesitate for a minute, but then, apparently making an effort to sound friendly, she says, "No, it's all right. But I'd better just meet you at the train station. Then I can show you my studio on the way, if you like."

"Sure, sounds great . . . Um, who should I be looking out for?" Sven asks awkwardly.

"Oh, um . . . Right, so I'm thirty-one, blond, medium height, on the thin side, and today I'm wearing jeans and a tan corduroy blazer."

"Okay, so I'll see you at the train station. Thanks!"

"No problem. Bye!"

"Yeah, bye!" Sven hangs up. He can't help grinning, happy that he will finally get his chance to meet Clara in person. He tosses the kid's phone back to him and quickly marches off to find the departures board to look for the next train.

clara

*H*opefully *it's not a bad sign that this Lehmann guy is so late,* Clara thinks. After all, for all her self-doubt she still sees this interview as a way of helping herself launch her freelance career. But she got the impression that the guy was likable and down-to-earth, so she's happy about that. And he'd sounded younger than expected, on the phone at least.

Clara is a bit angry that she didn't just google him beforehand. If he works for such a prominent magazine there's bound to be a photo of him online somewhere. On the other hand, if he were even moderately attractive, then she was sure to have been even more nervous before the interview, Clara thinks as she crosses the street in front of the train station.

She hasn't been back here since winter. On Christmas Day Ben had gone with his mother and Dorothea to visit his grandmother near Düsseldorf. A few days later he took the train back—he had a gig with his band on New Year's Eve and wanted to be back in Lüneburg in time for rehearsal. Clara can still vividly remember picking him up at the station that day and how much she had looked forward to seeing him again, even though it had only been a few days that they'd spent apart after he proposed on Christmas Eve.

And yet Ben had been so strangely quiet that day. Maybe because even at this time he was already straining against the commitment he'd chosen to make. Was it already clear to him, even then, that he wouldn't be able to see it through?

Clara's throat tightens as she thinks now that Ben might have known that he was saying good-bye to his grandmother, who was so dear to him, for the last time. He probably spent the whole train ride staring out the window, filled with deep sadness. When he arrived in Lüneburg it must have taken an unbelievable effort for him to pull himself together so that Clara wouldn't suspect anything.

And now she's back here again—but everything is different.

It's like at Castello the other night, Clara thinks. *Everything I do now I'm doing for the first time—not with Ben, but alone.*

But ultimately it's Ben and Ben alone whom she has to thank for the fact that she's standing here now. Here, at this turning point in her life, which suddenly feels like a completely fresh start. From this point forward she's headed in a direction that she never would have dreamed of before. And she never would have imagined that she would be capable of choosing such a bold path.

Clara is still completely lost in thought when the Metronom commuter train from Hamburg finally arrives. Suddenly her mind is blank—all the clever lines that she'd spent the whole day preparing are gone, just like that. And before she can start looking for a man in a suit, she's already being spoken to.

"You must be Clara Sommerfeld!" says a terrifyingly good-looking man in jeans carrying a small laptop case.

"Uh, yes. Mr. Lehmann?"

He shakes her hand and looks so deeply into her eyes that Clara is completely discombobulated.

"Sven Lehmann, that's right. Thank you for waiting so long."

. . .

This guy just makes me nervous somehow, Clara thinks, sitting across from him now at Cheers at the very same table she and Ben sat at the night they met. What a strange coincidence that Mr. Lehmann would head for this table, even though there were several others available. But she likes the man; he's got a cool sense of humor and loads of charm, which he no doubt has expertly deployed on hundreds of women by now.

"It's a really good fit, you and this lovely little city," he had confidently declared as Clara closed the door to her studio behind her. During the brief tour she'd given him the journalist had also taken a few photos of her. She had simply ignored his compliment.

How old is he? Clara asks herself now as she studies his face on the sly. *Definitely somewhere around forty,* she thinks, and then quickly looks down at the menu again, even though she knows the selection of food and drinks here by heart.

"So how is it you're actually going to approach the topic of 'freelancers'?" Clara asks, determined to get through this conversation as capably as possible. Meanwhile, inside, she's admonishing herself to ignore the fact that the man she's speaking to exerts a certain fascination on her. The macho side of him that shows through in an occasional comment or gesture reminds her of Ben, and as soon as she realizes this, she starts to feel guilty. But she'll just act as professionally as possible and not leave her interviewer any room for personal chitchat.

Sven Lehmann readily explains how he's envisioning the article. And even though Clara is really interested, somehow she isn't
capable of fully listening to him. *No wonder,* she thinks to herself,
*with those eyes of his! Do the people at the next table think we're a couple?
But Beppo said he's with someone! In any case it definitely wasn't a colleague or a platonic friend who he was out for dinner with at Castello. Beppo's got an unfailing sense for these things. Does this Lehmann guy take his
girlfriend or wife or whoever she is to Lüneburg often?*

"I think I'm going to get a glass of the house white. How about
you? We could also get a whole bottle. It's my treat, of course."
He looks at her with a smile and a glint in his eye that makes
Clara feel all the more unsure of herself.

"Um, I'd rather have a spritzer . . . that is, a juice spritzer . . .
so sparkling water with passion fruit juice and not sparkling water with wine," Clara hears herself stammering. She feels like
biting her tongue—this sounds anything but confident and professional.

Lehmann also looks a bit puzzled, but when he places their
orders with the server, his voice sounds exceedingly casual and
charming again. He also comments smugly on her choice of
bar—"So, this is your favorite spot, is it?"—and flashes that rogu-
ish smile of his again.

Clara feels impelled to respond right away. "Yeah, I know, there
are trendier places, but I like the atmosphere here, and I guess
I'm just a creature of habit."

"A creature of habit who's also quite willing to open herself up
to something new, though, right?" the man across from her asks,
still grinning.

"Sure. But where being self-employed is concerned, at least, I
really don't have any other choice. If you work as a freelancer
you've just got to be flexible and also willing to, like you said,

open yourself up to something new," Clara replies and is very relieved that they've finally arrived at the topic that they're actually here this evening to discuss. She has no idea where to put her hands, so she just shoves them under her thighs, hoping the journalist won't notice how nervous this whole thing makes her.

"You're not cold, are you?" Lehmann asks with concern.

Clara only shakes her head. *No, it's just that you're making me feel so unsure of myself with your funny questions and those looks you keep giving me,* she thinks to herself.

"But I'll have to excuse myself for a second, if you don't mind," she says shyly.

"Of course not. Unless you're going to leave me here alone on purpose—as payback for being so late," he banters playfully.

Clara smiles awkwardly and feels herself blushing a little. She quickly flees in the direction of the bathrooms. She has this feeling that she urgently needs to send a text. To Ben.

sven

Shortly before midnight, when Sven drops his keys and his phone onto the dresser next to the front door of his loft, he sees that he's got a text. He looks hesitantly at the display. A text from Clara! But he doesn't know whether he should be happy or angry. After all, it's still not meant for him.

> Ben, I have a confession to make, which I'm sure you already know by now: I've cheated on you at our table and now I feel guilty. Please believe me, no one could ever replace you.
> Your L.

Sven can't help but wonder at the words "I've cheated on you"— and what's this about "our" table?

The whole ride back he had thought about how much he would have liked to touch this sensitive woman or at the very least to have showered her with compliments. She left him enchanted. But the looks she gave him and the gestures she made were all evasive; she immediately parried every attempt he made to get closer to her.

Sven had been on many, probably too many, dates without having anything to show for it except for the belief that over time he has grown better at deciphering the mysterious behavior of the opposite sex. Like when a woman props her chin on her hand and tilts her head to one side. In eighty percent of cases that means that when he takes the first step to cross the invisible border between them and reaches to carefully but firmly touch her other hand, flitting nervously across the table top between the coaster and the silverware, or her napkin and her glass, she won't pull it away. Or if she bends her chest slightly forward to better accentuate her breasts—that means that there's a very high likelihood of his being able to touch them at a later point in time.

But with Clara there was nothing! No hints, no signals, not a single gesture of interest. And it wasn't like she seemed cold or anything; she'd been just as friendly as Sven had always imagined her being. At the same time there was something unapproachable about her, which meant that the attraction Sven felt toward her from the first second only increased as the evening went on.

Just thinking of the way she'd stood there on the platform— bashful, like a little girl, and yet sexy, like a young woman who is fully aware of how attractive she is but isn't trying to make anything of it. At the memory of their first encounter there at the station, Sven can't help but sigh. But then he gets a hold of himself, puts his phone away, takes his shoes off, and tosses his jacket into the corner. He turns the TV on, grabs a beer from the fridge, and throws himself down onto the couch, laptop bag and all. Next he gets out the digital camera that he used to take pictures of Clara and her studio. Even though he'd looked at the photos incessantly during the train ride, he now feels the urge to look at them yet again.

And there he sees it again, this radiance in Clara's bright green eyes.

The sight of her so captivates him that he's tempted to just call her number right this instant. No more workarounds, no more business talk—totally direct and totally personal. He's just about to grab his phone, but then he freezes.

This last text is just the latest confirmation of the uncomfortable feeling he has that this woman is in love with someone else.

The best thing he could do, he decides, is to forget about her as quickly as possible.

clara

I f you had a man we wouldn't have to do all this heavy lifting,"
Katja says with a grin, waiting to get another rag thrown at her
by Clara.

"Okay, I get it. It's my own fault; I'm standing in the way of my
own happiness and am just an all-around hopeless case," Clara
responds sarcastically and lets out a groan as she attempts to lift
what is indeed a particularly heavy paint can out of her trunk.

"Do you think he would have kissed you if you hadn't com-
ported yourself like a refrigerator?" Katja keeps needling and
heaves the second bucket out of the car.

"It wasn't a date; it was a professional meeting that—"

"That could've gone a lot differently," Katja interrupts.

Clara sets down the paint can, draws herself up, and turns to
face her friend: "Okay, let's go over this again: First of all, the guy
is a serious journalist who—"

"Who asked you if you'd like to grab a drink sometime
because—and I quote—'it had been really nice!'"

Clara rolls her eyes and continues: "Second of all, the guy is
with someone already."

"But you don't have proof of that."

"I do have a reliable witness who described in no uncertain terms how attractive the woman with him at Castello was."

"So what? We thought Andy was married at first just because he had a ring on his finger!"

"Third of all, guys who are that good-looking are very good at getting their kicks with a woman in the short term. A guy like that doesn't want to really commit himself."

"You know he can't help it that he's good-looking."

"But he tried to hit on me!"

"Is it a crime for a man to act confident and in control and want to take what he likes?"

"No. More like . . . sexy," Clara has to admit."

"Aha!"

"Oh, don't you 'aha!' me. That's the problem right there. Because fourth of all: I'm not ready yet. And fifth of all: I'm concentrating on my career right now!"

"Which he could really help you out with . . ."

"That's why I've got you. Come on! The studio isn't going to paint itself."

Katja tries to respond, but she's already used up all of her arguments. Which leaves her only one last option: blackmail.

"All right, either you get in touch with him today or I'm not lifting a finger!"

Clara gives Katja a withering glare. But she can only hold it for about five seconds—then her lips twist up in a crooked grin that Katja, in her inimitable way, claims as a major victory.

sven

Well, if nothing else you've still got to call her to get her to sign off on the article," Hilke says encouragingly, like a caring grandmother who means well but hasn't got a clue.

"I'll do that over email," Sven replies, his face totally blank.

"Okay, and in the email you could gently hint that you would be . . . um . . . very interested in working with her again," she suggests, not sounding particularly convinced herself.

"I'm not going to go to pieces just because a woman turned me down. So don't go making a big deal of it. I only told you that we met because you would have found out about it anyway."

"But it is a big deal if you're just going to give up now!"

"Dear Hilke, this isn't a movie; this is real life, and in real life I've got a lot of work to do. So may I go back to doing my job, please?"

"Dear Sven, it doesn't matter if it's real life or the movies: You always have to fight for love."

"Says who?"

"Says me. Me and everybody else. And Clara for sure, as romantic as she is."

"Yeah, so romantic that she let me crash and burn like a race car smashing into a cement wall!"

"But you said she's attractive. And . . ."

"And what?"

"I take no pleasure in saying this. But you're also attractive."

Sven looks out the window, embarrassed. He's used to receiving insults from his colleague, not compliments.

"Mmm . . . But that hardly means that Clara is into me."

"What did she say again exactly?"

"I just told you that."

"You did not! Okay, fine, you did. But I have to know the *exact* words. We're talking about very small but subtle differences here!"

"Women! Okay, I politely said goodbye and said that it had been really nice and we could also do it again sometime without the interview if she wanted."

"And what did she say?"

"Nothing! She just smiled, wouldn't look at me, just like she hadn't looked at me during the whole conversation, and wished me a good trip home."

"Yeah, but that doesn't mean she turned you down!"

"This right here does," Sven says with a lot more of an edge in his voice and reaches for his phone.

When he shows Hilke Clara's last text, she's too embarrassed to say anything.

Even a hopeless romantic like his colleague simply has to realize on seeing these words that Clara is still way too hung up on her ex, thinks Sven. There just wouldn't be any point in pursuing her.

"You see," he says, "she feels like she's cheated, even though she never even looked at me!"

Hilke frowns, disappointed, and takes a deep breath. In a way, Sven is relieved—now at least she's finally letting it drop.

clara

Clara lies in bed unable to sleep. They'd spent the whole weekend fixing up the studio, and even though she was so exhausted she could barely stay on her feet, she still took Katja out to dinner at Castello Sunday night to thank her for her help.

Naturally her friend had to use the opportunity to pump Beppo for information about the journalist—and above all about the woman he was with. It was true that he couldn't say for certain that the two of them were a couple, but he couldn't convincingly claim that the opposite was true, either. After that Katja drove her so crazy with her matchmaking attempts that Clara finally promised to at least send Sven a text message.

Good thing she'd gone ahead and saved his number after he'd called to say he was going to be late.

Now Clara opens the Sent Messages folder on her phone for the third time that night to make sure that she didn't write something completely stupid. Something that wasn't clear enough, or maybe was too clear and would make him think he'd better not respond. She reads her words aloud and tries to imbue them with an unmistakably friendly tone, at least after the fact:

> Hello, I totally forgot to thank you for the invite. So: thanks! And if you're still up for it, I'd be happy to do it again next weekend. 😊 Yours, Clara S.

If only for politeness's sake he should have replied by now—or was my text maybe too direct after all? Clara wonders, cursing herself and the awful dating world, with all its little games and rules that she thought she'd never have to torture herself with again. With Ben it had all been completely different. When they first met at Cheers, he talked her into another date right there and then and wasted no time in trying to win her.

Clara looks through her sent messages again. Except for two texts that she sent to Katja, all the others went to Ben—and then of course the one to Sven Lehmann. In this moment she becomes bitterly aware of the fact that there's barely anyone left in her life whom she'd describe as a friend. It's like everyone always says: When a crisis hits, you find out who your real friends are.

At first all the people she knew would check in regularly and ask how she was doing. But now, after more than half a year, Clara doesn't want to be the one who brings awkwardness and sadness with her whenever she happens to reach out. And conversely, everyone else probably feels overwhelmed just trying to act natural around her.

Clara resolves that in the future, when she meets new people, she'll do everything she can not to let her past get in the way. She wants to be able to get to know a new man in as natural a way as possible and not immediately scare him off with her history.

Because with Sven Thursday night, at the train station, at her studio, and later on at Cheers as well—Ben was present everywhere. Above all when the journalist was looking around her studio and photographing her, in a strange way she had felt Ben close to her, almost as if he were signaling to her that she was in good hands.

But in his own way Sven Lehmann had also given her a feeling of intimacy and trust. And this even though he'd made her so nervous!

Maybe he just reminds me of someone, Clara thinks, without really being able to put her finger on it. *In any case, this someone isn't Ben*, she thinks, then she snuggles down deeper under the covers. Really, in a lot of respects, the guy seems to be the exact opposite of Ben. Clara asks herself if that's a good or a bad sign. But then she admonishes herself not to waste any more time thinking about it. The fact that he didn't even respond to her text shows how superficial he is. No doubt he asks one woman after the next if they'd like to "do it again sometime"—while the truth is he wouldn't even remember their first meeting.

* * *

The next day Clara receives confirmation that her opinion of Sven Lehmann was correct. She sits at her computer and forwards the email that just came in to Katja without comment. After all, this level of coldness and arrogance requires no further elucidation.

Dear Ms. Sommerfeld,

I'm attaching the finished article and would be grateful if you could provide your approval in a timely fashion.

Many thanks for the pleasant conversation, and all the best in your new freelance career!

Best regards,
Sven Lehmann

Clara doesn't know who she should be angrier at: this stuck-up jerk or herself. After all, she was the one who had tried to tell herself that there was something special going on between them that night. If they'd gotten together a second time, the encounter would in all likelihood have just been awkward and inconsequential. But still, to just not respond to a text, and then write as impersonal an email as possible—this, she feels, is simply an affront. This she just can't stand for!

If nothing else, she'll read the article hypercritically and beat Mr. Lehmann over the head with every word she doesn't like.

Only now does Clara see that the attached article also includes photos. She had almost forgotten about them. There are photos of other freelancers in the article as well, a woman and two men who have likewise ventured to make the leap to self-employment this year. Clara is surprised that she's the only one pictured twice. And she's amazed how well some of her paintings and her sign come across, even though everything is just lying scattered about on the floor of her studio. Sven Lehmann was right that these were just the photos he needed: images that showed the persons portrayed in the starting blocks, so to speak.

Clara has to grin in spite of herself when she reads the caption:

Clara S. in her newly rented studio and shop
Art & Praxis: "A fair amount of naivete and appetite
for risk are just part of the mix."

Did I really say that? Clara asks herself, and before she knows it she's searching her memory of the stimulating exchange with the witty scribbler at Cheers that night.

He had called her a "refreshingly naive but shrewd and interesting artist."

After briefly objecting to this characterization, Clara had added honestly: "An artist who clearly doesn't understand much about business."

That got a hearty laugh from him. Really both of them had done a lot of laughing, well into the night, whether they were talking about the topic at hand or were off on one of the few digressions into more personal territory.

It did get weird though when Clara started talking about her paintings. Even though she had the impression that Lehmann was hanging on her every word, his response was very muted when she admitted that her moon series had a very personal element that she would prefer not to talk about.

He'd given her such a strange look then, as if he was just about to confess something very intimate to her. But in the end he just admitted that he knew next to nothing about art, and yet nevertheless—or maybe all the more so because of this—he was impressed by the power of her canvasses.

And so now Clara is very anxious to see what language he chooses to describe her work in the article.

First she skims through the text, only to take her time and read through it again line by line, even if it means giving up her lunch break to do so.

A short while later she is both relieved and at the same time disappointed that the so-called beginner's enthusiasm of the four entrepreneurs profiled isn't at all reflected in the tone of the article. It remains bone dry throughout—the kind of piece that only someone like Sven Lehmann could write.

Without waiting for Katja's reaction, Clara goes ahead and hits Reply.

> Dear Mr. Lehmann,
>
> Thank you for the objectively faultless article, which I'm happy to approve.
>
> I likewise wish you all the best for the future in both your professional and personal life!
>
> Yours sincerely,
> C. Sommerfeld

She hits Send and forwards this email, too—again without comment—to Katja.

. . .

The days remaining until the official opening of her studio are going by in such a blur that Clara is more than happy to have some time away from the agency. Not that there's any play involved. The list of things that have to get done by next Sunday seems endlessly long and would be impossible to get through without her mother and Katja's help.

"So, I'm not trying to be annoying or anything, but tell me," Katja says one evening as she's looking through the list of people to invite, "why isn't Sven Lehmann on here?"

"I thought you weren't trying to be annoying . . . ," Clara says without looking up from her stack of envelopes.

Her friend knows that trying to have a discussion at this moment would be pointless and reluctantly backs down. "Okay, then give it here; I'll do it. You worry about your paintings. But hold on! What are all these names? I don't know these people. Are these your coworkers?"

"Yeah, I'm killing two birds with one stone. I'm just going to tell them that the opening is doubling as my going-away party from the agency. Plus a few of them have really helped me out a lot."

"I see, got it."

"Not as much as you, of course!" Clara calls out before disappearing into the next room to hang her paintings.

"Mm-hmm, and sometimes you just have to keep on helping people, otherwise they'll never find happiness," Katja says so quietly that Clara can't hear. Then she stuffs an invitation into one of the unaddressed envelopes and drops it into her purse on the sly.

sven

Ugh, finally," an agitated Hilke greets her favorite colleague as he walks into the office.

"Morning, morning. What's up?" Sven asks, still half asleep.

"You've got mail!" Hilke says momentously and points to Sven's desk. "From Lüneburg!"

"I see," Sven grumbles and goes off to get a coffee, knowing full well that it will make Hilke livid.

"All right, open it already. Chop-chop!" she demands when he returns a few minutes later and holds a silvery-blue envelope right under his nose.

Annoyed, Sven tears the envelope open and scans the few lines printed on the paper within. As soon as he's done he drops both paper and envelope right into the wastebasket.

"Are you nuts? What does it say?"

"It's just an invitation."

Hilke stares at Sven, aghast.

"To the opening of her studio." Sven turns brusquely to his desk and turns on his computer.

"And you don't want to go?"

"Why should I?"

"Because it's impolite not to go."

Sven looks at Hilke like she's a small child who has just said something incredibly dumb.

"And because it's nice of Clara Sommerfeld to invite you," she adds meekly.

The look on Sven's face is unchanged.

"And besides," Hilke ventures another attempt, "what do you have to lose?"

"My heart," Sven mutters softly and stares at his screen.

Hilke walks over to the wastebasket, fishes out the letter, and reads through the invitation.

"Hey, you know what? We'll just go there together," Hilke says happily, already looking forward to it, and nods euphorically at her colleague.

Sven bangs his head against his desk melodramatically. "What have I done to deserve this?"

clara

C lara takes a moment to type a quick text to Ben before the excitement of today really gets going. Her mother and Reinhard are already here, as well as Lisbeth and Willy. Katja and Andy still haven't shown, of course. *But the person whose absence is most glaring,* Clara thinks, *is Ben.*

She doesn't really know if she should be laughing or crying, and she hopes that texting him real quick will calm her down a little.

> My darling, I'm so insanely excited, but so thankful, too. And even though I'm missing you so incredibly much today, I know that you're still here all the same. Thank you!

The invitation Clara sent out listed an eleven o'clock start time, but it's already half past eleven and there's still only a smattering of people in the two rooms of the studio. Every now and again, though, people she doesn't know stop in.

On this rare Sunday when the shops are open, the people are

flocking to the city in droves and filling even the side streets. Anyone who'd like one gets a glass of prosecco or orange juice, plus canapés. Despite Clara's vehement protestations, Beppo had insisted that today's catering was a housewarming gift.

Clara steps away from a small group of former coworkers to pause for breath for a few seconds and take in this unreal moment.

She really appreciates it that Niklas and his wife have come. It wasn't easy for her former boss to let her go. Things still aren't going well at the agency. But everyone congratulates her on her talent and also on her courage. And even if things have been changing so fast in the past few weeks and it all still seems a bit strange, deep down Clara continues to feel that this is the right move.

She's just about to leave the side room gallery and head back down the half flight of stairs to the main room when her heart skips a beat.

Sven Lehmann is here! He and an attractive brunette have just started mixing among the crowd of what must be about twenty people at this point. Six or so feet behind them Clara can see that Katja and Andy have finally arrived as well.

Katja seems to be hiding behind her boyfriend so as to be able to observe the arrival of the new guests as closely as possible. Clara casts a glare her way as she slowly walks down the stairs.

Katja gives a sheepish shrug, walks over to Clara, and says, her face flushed with nervousness: "Okay, guilty as charged. This was entirely my doing. But only where he's concerned. I don't know what the floozy is doing here!"

The woman with Sven not only looks pretty, Clara thinks, *she also seems totally likable, unfortunately*—which of course you couldn't say about Mr. Lehmann at the moment. It's true that the brown corduroy jacket he's wearing suits him really well, but he's got a pretty bored expression on his face as he looks around the room.

That arrogant jerk, Clara groans. His girlfriend is at least paying attention to the paintings on the walls.

"Well, go on already!" Katja orders with a certain bluntness, but only because they both know Clara doesn't have a choice.

"Uh . . . hello," Clara greets the surprise guest and offers her hand to shake. "How nice that the two of you are here." As she utters this lie, Clara looks at Sven's attractive companion.

"I'm Hilke Schneider, Sven's colleague—and your biggest fan!" says the brunette with an enthusiasm that sounds quite sincere.

"Clara Sommerfeld. Thanks very much! Would you like a little something to drink?" Clara gestures over to Katja, who is just then making the rounds with a tray of prosecco and clearly having fun attending to the guests.

"Sure!" Hilke says, at the same time Sven says, "No thanks." Clara looks first at one, then at the other, and suddenly all three let out an embarrassed laugh.

"Just a sec," says Clara and waves Katja over.

"Yeah, so, um . . . thanks for the invite," Sven Lehmann says a bit awkwardly as Clara takes a glass of prosecco from the tray and hands it to his colleague.

"You're welcome. May I introduce my friend—and at least part-time business partner—Katja Albers? Katja, this is Hilke Schneider and Sven Lehmann."

"So you're the one who wrote that great article?" Right away Katja engages the two guests in a conversation. Soon enough Andy joins in as well, and the four of them start chatting away. But Clara isn't in the mood for small talk. Plus she has to look after the other guests.

There are some questions that Clara hasn't even started to think about how to answer yet. Like where she gets her ideas; if the Lüneburg scenes are available as a calendar or coffee mug; if there's a catalog; and when she would start offering painting classes, which had already been mentioned in the local paper.

About an hour later Hilke comes up to Clara to ask about a painting that she'd like to buy but that doesn't seem to have a price tag next to it. They quickly agree to a sum that is much larger than Clara expected it would be. Hilke Schneider on the other hand seems like she can hardly believe her luck.

"All right, now I get to head home with a real bargain," she says and gives Clara a very warm smile. Then she suddenly adds: "By the way, I was lying to you earlier . . ."

With a mischievous look on her face she glances over at Sven Lehmann, who is still chatting excitedly with Andy and Katja. A shudder goes through Clara's body—she knows what's coming. In less than five seconds this hellishly attractive woman is going to confess to her that she and Sven Lehmann aren't just colleagues but also a couple. She's probably seven weeks pregnant and about to step before the altar with her darling man.

"Uh . . . oh?" Clara asks, not sure how to respond.

"I do really like your paintings. But *I'm* not your biggest fan. That title goes to someone else . . . ," Hilke says with a smile and casts another meaningful glance over at the others. Then she announces politely that she has to get going now—but with a friendly wink, she wishes Clara all the best for the future.

Clara follows her, half dazed, so that she can say goodbye to Sven as well.

"So, yeah, um . . . your colleague just said she was about to head out." Clara cuts into the conversation, hoping ardently that the general hum of voices will cover up how shaky her voice sounds. As Hilke Schneider heads for the door carrying her painting, Katja and Andy discreetly step back and go help themselves to some prosecco.

"I'd actually had something very different in mind for the next time we saw each other," Sven says all of a sudden, his tone fairly blunt.

"Oh yeah? Different how, if I may ask?"

"Well, fewer people around, for one thing."

"Aha, so you *are* interested in meeting up again after all?"

"What do you mean 'after all'? I did say I'd like to do it again sometime. I can't remember ever rescinding my statement."

"But you didn't insist on it, either."

"Well, okay then: I insist!" Sven can't believe he just said this.

"So what do you propose?" Clara can't believe she just said this.

"Well, just that: Let's do it again sometime."

"Good, then how about next Friday? Meet at the train station—the same late train, the same bar, the same white wine. Only this time I'll be drinking and I get to ask the questions!"

"Is that a promise or a threat?" Sven asks and gives Clara a teasing look.

"Both!"

They smile at each other and say goodbye, shaking hands again. It seems to Clara that, unlike a normal handshake, their hands remain touching for about two pleasantly tingling seconds too long.

sven

That Friday evening, with butterflies in his stomach, Sven heads for the not very inviting train bathroom for the third time. The conductor just announced that Lüneburg was the next stop, but he just can't bear it any longer.

When he looks into the mirror, he asks himself if it wouldn't have been better after all to wear a button-down shirt instead of a sweater. But Hilke—not that anyone had asked her—had been adamant that Clara was definitely more into the laid-back type and not the stuffy office twerp. Hilke also approved of his choice of aftershave. Until that moment Sven had been entirely unaware of the fact that his colleague even knew he wore aftershave. But now he's wondering if he might have put too much on.

The mere thought of sitting across the table from Clara again fills him with a feeling of nervousness that he simply cannot let show when they first see each other. He'd better start out with a compliment that totally floors her right from the outset and makes clear that he's so entranced at the sight of her that he's not fully in command of his senses.

clara

C lara stands waiting at the train station, weak in the knees, and wonders if this date is actually about to happen. No text, no email, no phone call—since last Sunday there had been no contact, nothing at all that she could seize on as proof that the conversation she'd had with Sven Lehmann after several glasses of prosecco would actually lead to a date.

The station loudspeaker has just announced that the train from Hamburg will be arriving shortly. It's exactly like last time, only this time she's not just nervous, she's super-mega-nervous. This time she's not just worried about what she's going to say, she's also even more worried about how she looks.

Five times she had sought Katja's assurance that a pair of jeans and a simple, casual top would really be the right outfit for this evening. Katja also told her on the phone not to overdo it with the makeup—he's sure to be more into the natural type. Her heels, on the other hand, should be on the high side, since otherwise if he tried to kiss her she would barely come up to his Adam's apple.

The mere thought of this makes Clara's heart beat twice as fast. She'd rather not even try to imagine anything beyond that. She decides to send another reassuring text to Ben really quick, because if she doesn't she's worried she'll collapse right there on the spot.

> Oh, Ben, you'll always be in my heart. No matter what happens tonight. I promise!

. . .

Eyes closed, Clara breathes in slowly, relishing the aroma of fresh coffee. She stretches out on her magnificently soft couch and surrenders herself to the warm feeling that fills her entire body. It must be the weekend!

Oh God! But what's going on? Why does she smell coffee and hear the sound of her coffee machine gurgling away? What are those rummaging noises in the kitchen? And where did this funny feeling in her stomach come from? This feeling like her life has gone from black-and-white to color and from cold to warm? But more than anything she asks herself: *How'd I get this pounding headache?*

Right, it was probably all the carafes of pinot grigio and the bottle of sparkling wine that she and Sven opened when they got back to her apartment late last night.

Clara tries to recall all the wonderful moments from yesterday evening and the ensuing night, letting them play out in slow motion before her mind's eye. Are her disjointed memories really accurate? Or could something horribly embarrassing have happened?

Did I say anything about Ben? Clara asks herself—and in an instant she's sitting bolt upright. But she's pretty sure that aside from mentioning her past a few times in a vague way, saying only that it was difficult and often still very present in her mind, she had avoided, as best she could, putting Sven off with her gloomy life story.

She does remember, though, going to the bathroom for the last time at the bar, looking at her reflection in the mirror, and trying to be strict with herself, grinning all the while and slurring her words, saying she must not, under any circumstances, take Sven home with her. But somehow, a short time later, they were marching off not in the direction of the train station but of her apartment. Clara quickly went from room to room in her head trying to think if there were any reminders of Ben in view. But most of the mementos were hidden in drawers, closets, or boxes anyway. If there was anything like a shrine to his memory, it was only in the bedroom. There was the photo on her nightstand, the song lyrics on the corkboard, an unwashed T-shirt, and the duvet cover on the left side of the bed that she'd never changed . . . All very good reasons not to let things go that far and to make Sven spend the night on the couch.

There's still a banging and clattering to be heard in the kitchen, though it's not particularly loud, as if Sven were trying very hard not to wake her. Clara isn't sure if she should get up, walk to the kitchen, and put her arms around him from behind or stay on the couch and let herself be surprised.

She pulls the wool blanket up over her nose, closes her eyes, and enjoys the feeling of simply knowing that someone is there. Just like she did all night long. It was simply wonderful—this mix of tingling excitement and a strange sense of familiarity.

First their hands had brushed against each other on the table, seemingly by accident. And later, on the couch, as they lay wrapped in each other's arms, simply holding each other, it was as if a spell was lifted. A spell that Clara didn't even know had been in effect. And even if she would have liked to give herself to Sven and enjoy to the fullest the wonderful sensation of feeling desired and at the same time protected, last night it was much more important to her to just enjoy being close to him and feel his gentle breathing on her neck, until at some point in the early hours of morning, nestled closely against each other on the couch, they had fallen asleep.

sven

On the way home from the train station, Sven thinks constantly of Clara, of her shining eyes and the sensuality she radiates—but he also, suddenly, has to think of David. Just a few months ago he thought his buddy was nuts for making such a big deal about meeting a woman. And now, clearly, the same thing had happened to him.

I'm head over heels, he thinks. And everything that was unimaginable to him a short time ago suddenly seems within easy reach. Like a path laid down in advance—there's no other road to take.

Even if he would have gone to bed with Clara the moment he got to Lüneburg if he could have, and even if the mere thought of sleeping with her fills him with a feeling of deep desire, he actually thought it was very sweet how she had held back—and held him back, too.

And really he felt like he needed to first take in every word she spoke, every gesture, every smile. As if he first had to bring to life, one by one, all the fantasies that he had formed in connection with Clara. Even if in her circumspect way she already seemed so familiar to him, every time he actually saw or touched this woman, a new world opened up, a world he wanted to explore down to the last detail. The less Clara revealed about herself, the stronger the need within him grew: the need to know everything about her. Yesterday she had been very guarded in speaking of her past. Sven had to be careful not to let himself get carried away and say something he shouldn't have. He'd been able to find an at least halfway plausible-sounding explanation for the mix-up involving the text that Clara, thinking that she was texting him, had sent to the money-grubbing teenager from the Altona train station. She seemed to believe his story, at any rate. After working so hard to gain her trust, he didn't want to lose it again right away. And so he just claimed that the phone he'd called her from was his work phone, which he only carried with him for appointments outside the office, otherwise he just left it in a drawer in his desk and ignored it. Sven is just lucky that Clara didn't immediately ask for his personal cell phone number. In that poignant, romantic moment on the couch, it would have been impossible for him to invent a good reason why he couldn't give it to her right then and there.

But Sven knows that he can't leave Clara in the dark forever. By the time they see each other again next Friday in Hamburg, he'll think up a way that he can tell her the whole truth, a way that's gentle but direct, so that there's nothing standing between them.

With this resolve firm in his mind, he now runs up the stairs to his apartment. Right as he's about to toss his jacket over the back of the sofa, his phone dings.

Sven first has to grin, but then he starts to feel a bit of a lump in his throat when he reads the text from Clara:

> Oh Ben, I'm so happy, but I'm dying of guilt. Even if I'm on the verge of falling in love with someone else, I'll never forget you!

The more distance there is between now and last night, and the more miles he's put between him and Clara, the more doubts begin to assail Sven. What if she can't bear the truth? Will she still look at him so dreamily once he's confessed everything to her? Has he gotten himself into a hopeless situation? What if the attraction between them, which he'd thought was so plainly apparent at breakfast together this morning, was just wishful thinking?

Sven reads the text over and over again. Feeling unnerved, he decides to call Clara today and finally tell her everything.

As he's headed to the kitchen—first things first, he's going to make himself a cup of coffee—his telephone rings. Aside from his father, almost no one he knows still takes the trouble to call his landline. Most people either call his cell or get in touch by email.

Sven looks at the caller ID. Seeing that it's a Lüneburg area code, he takes a deep breath, picks up, and says cheerily: "Hello, beautiful!"

"Hmm. Who might this 'beautiful' be, I wonder?" asks a skeptical but oh-so-familiar voice.

"For me there's only one woman in the world worthy of the name."

"All right. I guess I'll believe you. But who knows?" Clara says teasingly. "Maybe you're leading a double life . . ."

"Now why would I do that? Besides, if I were then I certainly wouldn't have invited you over to my place."

"Mmm, okay. You win this round. But how come I have to look your number up in the phone book?"

"Well, you know, I'm not going to serve you up all my secrets on a silver platter. You're going to have to earn them, one by one!"

"And how do I do that, if I might ask?"

"Oh, the terms of the exchange are pretty fair. I provide secrets, you provide tender kisses, soothing neck massages, gentle caresses . . ."

"Right, right, and I'm sure you can think up a lot more besides that."

"Oh, sure." Sven can't help but smile. "I had a really great time yesterday."

"Me, too," he hears Clara whisper into the receiver. And then she asks: "What's all that racket you're making?"

"I was just about to make myself a cup of coffee. Come on over, I'll make you one, too."

"Now don't you start that again, you know I'm—"

"Up to your ears in work. Can I help you with anything?"

"No, stop it. Besides, you already helped me more than enough with the article you wrote. And that wasn't even the best part about meeting you."

Sven can't help it; he's just standing there grinning. He reaches for his favorite mug, fills it with coffee and a little milk, and heads for the couch to kick back and relax with his coffee and Clara's voice.

clara

Clara can still hear Sven's voice in her ear after their long phone conversation. And really all she'd wanted was to say a quick hello to Sven and then head to the studio to keep working on all the stuff that still urgently needed taking care of.

It was Katja who urged her to call Sven. And now Clara feels even more strongly that her sense of things is correct. This man is really serious about her!

But now half of Saturday is already gone, and Clara just can't concentrate at all anymore. Finally she decides to take a break. She'll go on a long walk and drop in on her grandparents.

There are so many thoughts to get in order. Clara feels like she could walk around the entire world and she still wouldn't be able to sort out the buzzing chaos in her head. Everywhere she looks she's reminded of Sven. Everything that seemed hopeless and full of despair just a few days ago has suddenly brightened up, and she can barely even remember this dark and crippling feeling. She feels more like she's in a bright, colorful movie, where she's playing the leading role but can still sit back quietly and enjoy watching the action unfold.

Even Katja has taken to claiming in recent days that when true love reveals itself, it does so in more of a calm, quiet way. And she's also got a good example handy: Even if she's seeing everything through rose-colored glasses at the moment on account of Andy, still, she says, for the first time in her life there's a sense of calm inside her. A wonderful sense of calm. As if she had found peace.

Clara couldn't follow Katja at first when her friend was talking about how she felt. She just couldn't understand what was supposed to be so different about this thing with Andy as compared to the emotional roller coaster she went through with that guy Robert. Couldn't it be over just as quickly? Robert had disqualified himself once and for all after Katja tracked down his wife and asked her fairly directly if the divorce Robert had claimed was imminent was really happening. It was the first the wife had heard of it. That settled things for Katja. She almost seemed relieved that after many long weeks of suffering the worst had finally happened and it was finally over with. After that at least she had certainty.

Thinking about it now though, Clara feels she understands what Katja meant when she talked about her new attitude toward life. By this point the change in her friend's personality is so complete that when they were talking on the phone earlier, she had mentioned something—just in passing, casual as could be— about wanting a child. But because Clara was so focused on telling her about her night with Sven, she's only now realizing the significance of what her friend said.

Clara thinks about whether she should open up about her date to Lisbeth. But somehow the timing doesn't seem right yet. She'll get to meet Sven properly one day, anyway, Clara is sure of it. And if everything keeps going as wonderfully as it feels like it's going now, this opportunity is sure to come very soon. Clara is in no hurry. She just wants to sit back and let it all happen. She feels a newfound confidence that most things in life might turn out all right after all, and this feeling alone is enough to fill her with a profound and overwhelming sense of gratitude.

sven

How could I ever have forgotten how fun it is to cook? Sven asks himself as he proudly samples his filling for the grilled tomatoes. He plans to serve them with shrimp, a sliced baguette, and champagne when Clara arrives, which should be any minute now. He's already set out tea candles and transformed his roof terrace into a dazzling sea of light. He hopes to make her feel welcome and truly comfortable.

He's going to have to pick up the pace a little though. There are still a few things that need to be put away, like for example the tube socks in the corner or the *Playboy* on the nightstand, not to mention the bits of toothpaste that need to be scrubbed off the bathroom sink. He is after all assuming that Clara is going to spend the night with him.

In every one of their phone conversations since last Saturday there had been little suggestive hints, and Sven is truly feverish with expectation for their date tonight.

If she's on time and manages to find a parking space right away—which is unlikely—she could be ringing the buzzer just five minutes from now and be at the door a minute after that. Just as Sven is about to look to see if he can spot her trying to park from the terrace and come up with a few macho lines to have at the ready, his doorbell rings.

Heart pounding, he walks quickly to the entryway of the loft and energetically pulls open the door. There before him stands Clara, enchanting and bursting with life, wearing a knee-length summer skirt and a jean jacket, underneath which Sven can see a skin-tight, light-green T-shirt. Sven catches a brief glimpse of the seductively low-cut neckline, and what he sees is more than promising.

"Wow!" says Sven, inviting her inside.

"Wow!" says Clara, stepping into the loft and looking around. "I never would have thought you had such good taste." She flashes a grin at Sven and kisses him, fleetingly, but tenderly, on the mouth.

Sven wishes he could stop time to truly appreciate this moment and enjoy it more intensely. But he tries to act as casual as he can and says, "Well, if didn't have such good taste, I doubt I'd be thinking about you all the time."

Clara smiles, blushing, and Sven can't quite gauge if she's just being coquettish or if she is in fact this easily unsettled by compliments. He's so eager to find out more about her. There are so many questions; he wants to learn all the answers, one by one.

"And it wouldn't smell so good in here, either!" Clara adds and looks eagerly around.

First Sven takes her jacket from her and then he leads her by the hand through his domain and out to the terrace, where the table is set.

"I hope you're hungry!" he says, trying to mask his nervousness.

Clara looks at him, again blushing a little, and replies, "Sure, but to be honest I'm almost a bit too excited to eat anything right this second."

She takes a step closer to Sven and gazes at him intensely. Once more it's her eyes that move him so deeply, that make him just want to hold her in his arms. He smiles and lifts his hand as if to say: Don't move. He quickly hurries off to the kitchen to get the champagne, which he's been keeping extra cold. On the way back his eye catches the Pink Floyd record sleeve next to his record player. He quickly puts it back on the shelf with the other records and puts on a CD of light, catchy piano pieces. Finally he walks right up to Clara, wraps his arms around her, and whispers: "Come here."

He places one hand on the back of Clara's neck, so that for a time her head is resting against his chest. She looks up again and their lips come together in a long, intense kiss.

· · ·

Two hours and many kisses later, the bottle is empty. All the freshly grilled shrimp have been polished off. Sven spared no effort, serving Clara her meal with affection. Every bite was a kind of reward for her gamely answering one question after the next. Nevertheless she kept stressing again and again that on a night like tonight she'd rather look ahead into the future rather than backward, and that actually it was his turn to give an interview.

After slipping inside for a moment, Sven returns with a wool blanket and a bottle of white wine. He pulls out the footrest of his beach chair and reclines the backrest as far back as it will go. He gestures invitingly for Clara to sit and drapes the blanket over her with care.

"Voilà! The planetarium is open," he says ceremoniously and

not without a bit of pride. He sits down next to her, slips under the blanket, and puts his arm around her. As Clara readily snuggles up against him, he adds, "You see all those stars up there? That's how many questions I still have for you!"

Sven notices her pulling back a little and giving him a skeptical look.

"Okay, you can keep asking your questions, Mr. Star Reporter. But I reserve the right to decide whether I'm going to answer them truthfully or not. And also, we're going to take turns—after every question you ask, I'm going to ask you one!"

"Sounds good to me. But I get to go first," Sven declares. "Ms. Sommerfeld, all your adoring fans out there are dying to know: Why is it that you have such a hard time revealing interesting details about your personal life?"

Clara lets out a mock groan and answers sarcastically: "Well, you know, a successful artist needs her secrets. They're part of the aura of inspiration that surrounds her." She grins triumphantly and continues: "And you, Mr. Acts-like-he-wears-his-heart-on-his-sleeve-when-really-he's-just-a-playboy? Why do you have such a hard time revealing intimate details from your past? Hmm?"

Sven clears his throat and is tempted to give some witty made-up response. But he finally wants to make good on his promise to himself and not keep anything from Clara any longer. On the contrary, he wants to encourage her to be open about her own story. An experience like losing someone you love has a huge impact on a person's life; she shouldn't have to keep that experience to herself.

And so he urges himself to tell her only the truth from here on out. "First of all, I'm not a playboy, and I only speak about matters of the heart with people I trust. You're someone I trust, and so I'll tell you that I had almost lost faith in love, because it once let me down pretty bad . . . that'll have to do for now. Now it's my turn again: What do your paintings mean to you? What do they express?"

Clara sits up a little, and now Sven is angry at himself because he senses that he's gone too far. He has to proceed a little more gingerly from now on.

"More than anything, my paintings give me hope. Hope that all this striving to lead a good life has a deeper meaning, a meaning that I lost all sense of not too long ago . . . so, and now it's my turn again: What gives you hope?"

Sven can't help smiling, because really there's only one answer to that one—Clara! But he makes an effort to give her a more informative reply.

"Like I said, I'd almost given up hope myself. But ever since you came into my life, I've felt this vitality that I never knew existed before."

"Oh sure," Clara responds, "but you can't have been that comatose if all it takes to bring you back to life is a little game of question and answer!"

Sven is quite aware that this is Clara's clever way of probing for compliments. He's more than happy to turn on the charm; he knows what she's all too eager to hear, and it's not like it would be hard for him to come up with anything. But he really doesn't want to let this opportunity slip by without taking advantage of it; he doesn't want to get himself caught up in more lies that could shatter his dream.

"Well, you know, the thing is, I heard your wake-up call much earlier than you might think," Sven continues, feeling his way along. He knows that this is his chance to confess everything to

Clara. Finally he can tell her how long she's been in his life, and how much her presence has meant. "So, okay, it's like this . . . I have to . . . ugh, no, seriously now. I've fallen in love with you. It was the melancholy side of you that I fell in love with first. You have this way with words that I find so moving."

Clara caresses his face and smiles happily at him.

And so he continues: "And I love the natural, lighthearted side of you, which is so radiant with life. When you're painting or when you're writing as well . . . take the name Lilime, for example. That alone. Where does it come from, anyway? That's one question that I'm burning to know the answer to," says Sven, relieved that he's finally past the first hurdle on the way to the truth.

Clara sits bolt upright. Her eyes are blazing, but Sven can't figure out why she's reacting so strongly. "What is it? Did I say something wrong?"

Suddenly Clara's whole body is shaking. She starts looking around for her shoes.

"Clara, come on, tell me. What's going on?"

With a cold stare and trembling lips she snaps at him: "How do you know about that name?"

It hits Sven like a bolt of lightning. Lilime! How could he be so stupid? He couldn't have chosen a more tactless way of starting his confession.

"I . . . okay, listen, I . . ."

"Nobody in the world knows about that name," Clara continues. "What is this, investigative journalism?"

Sven can't manage to say another word.

"I hope you at least had fun rummaging through my things behind my back!"

Clara jumps up, grabs her shoes and her bag in a frenzy, and heads for the door so quickly that Sven has no time to react, all he can do is call after her: "Clara! Clara, please, wait. Clara!"

But she never looks back. She slams the door behind her and is simply gone.

clara

The whole time she's been driving Clara's mind has been working in such a frenzy that it's not really clear to her how she actually got out of Hamburg so quickly. She has no memory of making the turn onto the highway to Lüneburg, and now she's almost there. Of course, she can barely read the signs because her eyes are so puffy, and the tears just keep on coming.

She's in a state of utter despair. *What am I supposed to do now?* she wonders—both right now, on this night that is beyond ruined, and just in general at this point in her life. *A life that Ben ruined*, she thinks bitterly, though her guilty conscience immediately makes her regret thinking such a furious, even hateful thought.

Without weighing the pros and cons of it, she follows the impulse to get off one exit later in the hopes that her mother will be home and will have time for her.

A few minutes later, Clara is relieved to see that there's a light on in the living room. She rings her mother's doorbell.

"Clara, honey, what's wrong?" Karin looks at her daughter in dismay and immediately wraps her arms around her.

"Oh, Mom, it's all so horrible!" Clara mumbles and buries her face in her mother's neck. She cries bitter tears.

"It's all right, honey; it's all right," Karin says quietly and gently runs her hand over Clara's hair. "Come on inside. I'll just let Reinhard know that you're here. And then I'll make you your favorite tea, and you can take your time and tell me anything you want. Okay?"

. . .

Though Clara had first fallen asleep on the living room couch earlier, exhausted from the strain of that evening and the intense conversation with her mother, and maybe also from everything else that she'd lived through and suffered through over the last few months, she's now lying wide awake in the bed in the guest room, where everything smells soothing and fresh.

Her mother's words are still sinking in, but the longer Clara thinks about them, the calmer she feels inside.

It felt so good to finally let loose and complain, unfiltered, about what a raw deal fate had given her. About how she still gets assailed by feelings of guilt with stubborn regularity. About how she put so much hope in a new love and it came to nothing. And about how this hope was clearly just a tiny life preserver in a giant ocean, anyway.

Her mother didn't understand at first that the problem wasn't really Sven's snooping around, or not the main problem anyway. On the contrary, Karin even defended his behavior, saying it only showed how much this man was interested in her—though of course her mother did have to admit that curiosity had its limits.

After this initial misunderstanding, Clara almost wanted to

clam up again rather than expose herself further and end up feeling even more alone and misunderstood. But in the end no further explanations were necessary, because all at once her mother was able to intuit what she was actually going through on the inside. She thought it was completely understandable that it was hard for Clara to form a sense of trust in another person, even if this person didn't just take off from one moment to the next because he found out how much she was still caught up in the past. She even understood her worry that Sven wasn't capable of truly committing to her and that the tingling feeling of infatuation she felt was only the euphoria of a fleeting passion.

Without being arrogant or presumptuous, her mother got straight to the heart of what was most weighing on Clara deep down: her understandable concern that she might not ever be able to trust someone again, as well as her outsized fear that her feelings would be taken advantage of and she'd once again end up being left stranded—powerless, alone, and abandoned.

And just as Clara began to wonder how much she even trusted her mother and her advice anyway, Karin introduced a new perspective into the conversation that Clara hasn't been able to stop thinking about ever since.

Clara had described how close she'd been to telling Sven the whole story about Ben. He'd just given her such a strong sense that he was truly falling for her. At that point, her mother cut in to ask what she actually knew about Sven's inner life. And suddenly Clara remembered, crystal clear, what he'd said about his own restored sense of hope. It had been brave of him to be so honest with her.

"Then you know how he feels now," her mother said then. "He was about to open up to you and let you get close to him. He revealed something about his past and how he felt inside, and then he had to sit there and watch you leave, just like that, without any explanation."

She spoke this plain truth without criticism. Her voice was entirely neutral, like a voice speaking to Clara through the mirror.

And now Clara has to think of Katja, too, who really always had trouble letting anyone truly get close to her. As if by some miracle, and despite suffering a huge disappointment, her friend found Andy, a man who seems to be making a more relaxed and less cynical person of her. Clara feels the soothing waves of acceptance gently wash over her as she feels herself reconciling with her fate. Suddenly it becomes clear to her that Katja's good fortune is founded on her own misfortune. If Ben hadn't left her, Katja wouldn't have made such a stubborn effort to set her up with another man—and might never have met Andy and fallen in love.

Clara smiles meekly in the darkness. Again she starts brooding over where Sven could have found out about the nickname Lilime. She goes through her apartment and also the studio in her mind, trying to think if he could have found some stray sheet of paper, a letter, a CD case, or whatever else while she was still asleep or otherwise not paying attention.

Then again, maybe he'd just looked through her cell phone to find out if she was playing the field. Maybe he wanted to know if he could trust her. If so it's possible he could have seen a text to Ben in her Sent Messages folder.

But her intuition tells her that Sven wouldn't do such a thing. And besides, he would hardly have opened himself up to her if he had. But if he did in fact happen to see one of the texts she'd sent to Ben, then Clara would feel even more of an urge to confide in him completely, to tell him everything as soon as possible.

Feeling significantly calmer and thoroughly satisfied with the conclusions she's reached, she decides to call him first thing to-morrow morning. Really she'd like to text him right this second, just like she's been doing with Ben whenever she absolutely has to get something off her chest. How frustrating that she doesn't have his cell phone number!

But suddenly Clara feels utterly euphoric. Maybe he's already tried to get in touch with her. Should she turn her phone back on? She'd turned it off when she hit the first red light in Altona to make it unmistakably clear that she didn't want to hear from him.

Clara tiptoes quietly out into the hallway, trying not to wake her mother and Reinhard. She looks around for her bag in the dark, grabs her phone, and steps out onto the balcony to take a deep breath before checking it.

With trembling fingers she types in her PIN and waits impatiently for the display to show that she has reception. And look at that! In the time since she turned it off she's received three missed calls and a text.

First Clara checks her voice mail. The calls are from Sven, who apparently tried to call her from his landline. But he didn't leave a message, Clara registers with disappointment. Nervously she goes to check her inbox.

But what's this? Clara can't believe what she finds there. It feels like her heart is going to burst with excitement.

She has a text from Ben . . .

sven

W*hew! That felt good*, Sven sighs quietly to himself. He's just getting back home after going for a long run along the waterfront.

Even though he'd slowed down to an easy jog for the last few yards, his heart-rate monitor suddenly starts beeping loudly as he's climbing the stairs. Really he should be in good enough shape by now that climbing a few stairs shouldn't be enough to make his pulse rise above 140 beats per minute, no matter how quickly he runs up them.

But now he's got objective proof of how much power Clara has over him and his heart. He's felt nothing but listless since she took off last night, and it was a struggle to get himself to work out this morning. But in order to at least get a little distance from the emotional turmoil he's been going through, he made a point of not bringing his iPhone with him. And now with every step he grows more and more excited—could Clara have gotten in touch? At the same time, though, Sven is frustrated that exercising clearly hasn't helped one bit.

But still, if nothing else his conscience is finally clear. After calling Clara three times on both her cell and her landline and getting no answer each time, he finally sent a text from his cell. He'd spent hours tinkering with it, weighing every word several times over. The draft that he'd saved weeks earlier had served as the starting point. But the text was also supposed to express how much he regretted not having sent it sooner. The fear of never really getting to know either Clara or Lilime is too much for him to bear.

But now there's nothing Sven can do but wait and see if and how she might respond. At the same time, deep down, he already has to start pulling back and slowly clearing away the rubble so that he doesn't continue suffering any longer than he has to. He can't let his heart bleed out completely this time.

When he finally makes it upstairs, after what feels like an eternity, it seems like he's moving in slow motion. Slowly and ponderously he drags himself to the kitchen counter, reaches for his phone and looks at the display.

Sven can hardly believe it. Suddenly he feels like his heart might finally give out. He's got a text!

He's got a text from Clara!

A weight the size of a giant cement block falls from his shoulders. If nothing else, she's written back. She's speaking to him. He can't really fathom it, but there's a big smile on his face and his shining eyes start to read:

> Dear confidante, thank you for your courage, your openness, and your patience. What do you think about setting up another interview? Clara

Sven counts the letters and spaces. There are 139 characters. No doubt Clara had thought long and hard about every single word. He immediately hits Reply and types:

> How about a long walk on the Elbe—long enough that at the end of it there are no painful questions left, only liberating answers? Sven

Not a minute goes by before an answer arrives.

> Sounds wonderful. I'll be waiting for you by the harbor tomorrow, 3 p.m. (sharp!) at the Kehrwiederspitze.

clara

As Clara is crossing the bridges over the Elbe she can't help thinking of the little paper boat that, theoretically at least, must have found its way through Hamburg and out into the North Sea.

Of all things, Sven had proposed a walk along the Elbe! It feels almost as magical as the fact that it was really Ben who had led her to Sven—and thus helped her come back to life.

Though she'd mentioned the texts to Katja and Dorothea in the beginning, Clara hasn't told anyone about them since, and she's almost afraid that no one would believe her if she did. But that's not important now. The only thing that's important now is what she believes.

But what she believes at this moment is that, in a very real earthly sense, she is going to be late. This isn't a ploy to get a little payback on Sven; on the contrary, in a sense she's making things up to him, in that being late it puts her at a strategic disadvantage. She would much prefer being able to wait casually on a bench somewhere near the St. Pauli piers, that way she could watch Sven as he arrived and started looking around, trying to find her. Oh, how she'd like to watch him from a safe distance.

To look on as he locked up his bike, this bike that he's talked about so much you'd think it was his best friend. Or maybe to watch him running his fingers through his tousled hair. Only too much would Clara like to watch from a distance to see what kind of figure he cuts when he walks. She can't really remember anymore. Ever since the first time they met at the train station they had always walked side by side and on the way to her apartment even arm and arm.

It's now five to three, meaning it's now impossible for Clara to get to the place where they'd agreed to meet in time. And even though she opts for the route that takes her through the Freihafen and HafenCity to avoid as many red lights as possible, it's already ten past three before she's even close to the Kehrwiederspitze. She has to maneuver her car into a tiny parking space, and it takes her several attempts to straighten out. The last thing she wants is to embarrass herself in front of Sven if he walks her to her car afterward, even less so if he gets in with her.

Walking quickly now Clara draws closer to the glittering water. The sun is shining, and clearly they're not the only ones who had the idea of taking a walk by the harbor today. That must be him over there, waiting on a bench and enjoying the home field advantage. Or maybe not? Try as she might to pick him out of the crowd, Clara just can't find him.

Nervous, she looks herself over again and runs her tongue over her teeth to make sure there are no lipstick stains spoiling her smile. She'd really like to run back to her car and use some of the breath freshener spray that she always keeps in the glove compartment.

When, after ten minutes, Clara still can't find Sven anywhere, she checks her cell just to be sure. He might have texted to let her know he'd be late. But just as she's about to open her flip phone, "Call From: Sven" pops up on the display.

Clara is now very happy that after hesitating at first she had dared to take the next step and replace Ben's name with Sven's in her Contacts.

"Where are you?" asks Clara and looks around searchingly.

"That's a nice blouse you've got on." Sven's voice sounds confident and triumphant.

"Oh, you sneaky . . . where are you hiding?"

"Good thing you're not wearing the same shoes you had on two days ago. They were definitely sexy, no doubt about that, but with those heels we wouldn't have gotten more than a half mile . . ."

"Oh, come on, where are you?" Clara's desperate longing grows ever more intense.

"Hey, I was on time!"

"And I wasn't. Sorry. But you can cut it out with the payback routine now and show yourself already."

"Turn around three hundred sixty degrees to the right and then a hundred eighty degrees to the left."

"Ha, ha. Very funny."

"Just testing you. I mean, it's not like you can park . . ."

"Oooh, you creep! I guess you like spying on young women, is that it?"

"Oh, sure. Especially when they're as pretty as you!"

Finally their eyes meet. Clara sighs and waves at Sven, who she now sees is over across the street. He's standing right across from her parking space, which suddenly looks gigantic from where she's standing.

Sven walks toward her and they both put their phones away.

Now their hands are free for a long, firm embrace. And when she feels Sven's touch Clara can't help it, she has to fight back a few tears, even though, or maybe because, her heart is flooded with warmth.

. . .

When, after many steps and as many words, they reach a spot on the Elbe where they only encounter the occasional jogger or person out for a stroll, Sven suggests they start making their way back.

"You seem to have something else planned for me today," Clara says and finally manages to smile again.

"Absolutely," Sven replies softly and gently runs a finger down her face.

"But there's one thing I still don't understand. Are cell phone numbers really reassigned so quickly these days?"

"You know, I did look into that."

"I see. Investigative journalism, right?"

"Exactly. But I still never found out the whole truth . . ."

Clara looks at Sven expectantly.

"I mean," he says, "it is a bit strange. Because actually old numbers are only reassigned after a waiting period of six months from when the contract was terminated. So I guess it was just a technical glitch that brought us together."

"Well, it was definitely a lucky coincidence, wasn't it?" Clara replies softly and looks thoughtfully out over the water. She breathes in deeply. And because today with Sven she was able to unburden herself of so many thoughts, thoughts that she had kept deep within her and that she had to struggle to bring to the surface—because she has gotten so much off her chest already today, she now dares to say these next words aloud, smiling contentedly as she speaks: "And who knows? Maybe it wasn't a coincidence at all."